IMMORTAL
envy

A.D. Justice

Cover Designer & Photographer: Cassy Roop, Pink Ink Designs
Model: Daniel Wells

ISBN-13: 978-1539036906
ISBN-10: 1539036901

For my love.

IMMORTAL *envy*

Two brothers.
Best friends.
Immortals.
One woman—the subject of their mutual obsession, but for very different reasons.
The end result will change the New York City vampire clan forever. Immortals can hold a grudge for a very long time.

Prologue

Ramses Barnett's Journal, 1786

The burning need to taste her overcame me as soon as I caught her scent on my nightly prowl. She led the way into the darkened alley, my excitement and thirst increasing with every step. The aroma of her blood stirred the savage animal deep inside me, and my night wouldn't be complete without having her. Once we were well out of from the main street, she turned and gave me her most seductive smile.

"Shall we take care of business before we get down to business?" she purred.

"Of course," I replied as I wedged the silver coin between the smooth skin of her ample breasts.

I hiked up her dress and wrapped my hands around her bare ass, sliding her back against the brick wall until she was waist high. It was the perfect height for fucking her while I sank my teeth into the throbbing vein in her neck. While her moans of pleasure filled the air, her inner muscles clamped around my dick, and my fangs drained her blood, we climaxed together just before her body slumped over, and death took her under. It's called "the dead of the night" for a reason.

But one is never enough for me. That's always been my problem. My downfall. My vice.

A vampire has to drink blood to survive, plain and simple. My cravings become insatiable at times. I find I must leave the city or risk being discovered because I can't control my urges. The various scents surrounding me blend into one delicious aroma and send me into a frenzy. My brother, Slade, pushes me to feed on animal blood, deep in the forests where I won't be discovered. At times, I heed his advice and disappear for weeks at a time, feeding and living as wild and free as I want. The large animals fill me beyond measure and stay my fangs for longer periods than humans do, but animal blood just doesn't have the same sweet taste as human blood. It doesn't fulfill the constant craving that drives my immortal obsession.

The vast wilderness that lies outside the main cities in America provides excellent coverage for our feeding habits. Skirmishes with the natives, along with tall tales of their increased activity in the outlying areas, easily explains the humans *who are missing, and their family members desperately search for them. The settlers haven't ventured too far westward yet, but I have. It's not my first choice, but I can survive on the blood of animals when it's forced on me.*

But tonight, I'm in New York, an up-and-coming new city that's thriving, growing, and has a heartbeat all its own. Its pulse is so much different from the places Slade and I have spent decades upon decades living in. The vitality of the people, the thick, crimson indulgence that flows through them warms me from the inside out...just a little vampire humor.

I'm determined not to make the same mistakes I made before we came to America. During the hundred years we spent in and around London, we watched the city and people change seemingly before our eyes. With so many people, the city became a living, breathing buffet, and I couldn't resist having seconds or thirds. For as long as I can remember, Slade has been the level-headed one. The one who looks out for our best interests and drives me to consider all angles before making a decision.

A complete contradiction in terms, but Slade inspires me to be a better person. He's my younger brother, but he's always had my back. He has cleaned up after me when my impulsive nature left so many dead bodies our true nature was dangerously close to being revealed. Not that he hasn't given me the tongue-lashing I needed every single time, but I've never doubted his love for me.

Ramses Barnett, Current Day

Reliving days gone by through reading my old journal used to be one of my favorite things. But not today. Now, it's much like a silver stake to my heart. Not that silver stakes to the heart will kill a vampire, but I remember how a broken heart feels to a human. The sharp sting of betrayal never leaves me. It's always in the forefront of my mind, of my thoughts, and my feelings.

Yes, a vampire has feelings—especially toward other vampires. Especially when other vampires are family. Especially when that vampire family member is my brother.

Especially when I'd give anything for that vampire brother to be dead to me, just so I could move on without this hanging over my head and my heart.

But I can't let it go. I can't forget my brother. I can't forget the betrayal. I can't forgive—it's just not in me.

The past came crashing back to me tonight like a rogue wave crashing on the shore, rolling over everything and leaving rubble in its wake. I caught the whiff of a lingering scent in the air that has eluded me for too many years. The craving that drives me, the obsession that owns me, the woman who haunts me. The blood aroma was so tantalizing, spellbinding, and addictive, I pushed my way through the throngs of people on the New York City sidewalks at midday to find its source. When I lost track of the scent completely at a street corner, I knew she must have jumped into a taxi and was out of my reach.

But at least now I know beyond a shadow of a doubt she's here.

While standing there on the street corner today, I vowed I would not rest until I've found her.

If it's the last thing I ever do, I will find her.

And I will make her mine.

That leaves me in my current frustrated state, reading my old journal entries and reliving painful events that awaken the animal inside me. With the fires of my anger stoked and my senses aroused past the point of no return, I can't avoid feeding and fucking tonight. Not necessarily in that order. Not necessarily one at a time. While my strength is second to none in many areas, denying myself a few carnal pleasures isn't one of them.

In a flash, I'm walking the streets, on the prowl for my unsuspecting victim. The blonde who's a little too tipsy to be out here alone, who temporarily got turned around on her way back to her hotel room, is perfect. I can read her mind as plain as if she's speaking to me. She's in town on business, her first trip to the Big Apple, and was hell-bent on taking in the sights with or without her coworkers.

She's giggling to herself because she's amused by her predicament. From a small town, she thinks she's safe with so many people still milling around in the city that never sleeps.

"You're looking for a little adventure in your life, are you?" I ask aloud but to myself. "I'll be glad to accommodate you, beautiful. This is a once-in-a-lifetime opportunity."

Lady Luck shines on me like a bright spotlight. A group of guys steps out of an alleyway and into her direct path. The predatory way they eye her from top to bottom stalls her footsteps, and she looks around nervously. I take the opening to swoop in to her rescue and quickly take my place at her side. With my arm wrapped around her waist, I smile down at her confused expression.

"You're walking too fast, my love," I tell her. "I told you I had to go back to the table to leave a tip for the waiter." Holding her gaze makes my point known, and relief floods her eyes.

"I thought you were right behind me, honey. I'm sorry. I guess I had one too many glasses of moscato, huh?"

With a light chuckle, I shake my head affectionately and kiss her cheek. From my peripheral vision, I see the group of young men watching us. From my dark powers, I hear their thoughts and their low murmurs of how they can dispose of me and take her back to their hangout. Their bravado makes me want to laugh out loud. One vampiric glance from me and they'll all shit their pants and run home to Mommy.

I fucking love this part.

"Hey, gorgeous," one yells to her. "What's your name, baby?"

She glances up at me, clearly scared, and I flash her a reassuring smile as I squeeze her to me. "Tell him your name, sweetheart."

"Jennifer," she replies.

"Jennifer, you need a real man, baby. Come on over here with me and ditch that pasty-white fucker."

His taunt is clearly meant to rile me up so I'll fight him while his buddies jump me from behind. Once they've pulverized me, they'll drag her off and rape her. She'll be mine tonight, but it won't be against her will. These young punks haven't learned the art of seduction yet.

Or the art of choosing their opponents wisely.

"I'm more man than you can handle, junior. You and all your boys combined, in fact."

His smile morphs into a smug smirk, and his little gang steps up, their chests puffed out. One begins cracking his knuckles, as if that's scary and threatening. Another one curls his fingers into a fist and smacks his other hand with it. I can't stop the wide smile that covers my face at his action, or the laugh that follows.

Now that I've thoroughly riled them up, it's time to have a little fun.

In a protective move, I gently push Jennifer behind me as if I'm her personal shield and bodyguard. The young thugs begin hurling expletives at me, threats of bodily dismemberment, and other humorous insults.

"I'll knock your dick in the dirt and stomp your face in, motherfucker!"

"Shit, you got a big mouth, man. I'm gonna knock all your fucking teeth out."

Sticks and stones, young ones. Sticks and stones.

Jennifer's face is buried in my back, and her fingers have a death grip on my jacket. I take this time to show my true self. My nearly black eyes become cobalt blue in a split second. My fangs protract as I bear my teeth. My facial features contort and become fierce, more defined, in an instant. My voice deepens, and I issue my threat to the now petrified group.

"One more word, I dare you. Say one more word in front of Jennifer, and I guarantee it'll be the last fucking word your ignorant mouths ever utter."

They scatter to the four winds, unable to speak a single word in retaliation.

No matter—I know where to find the four of them after I've finished with Jennifer. They're too frightened to tell anyone, and they know no one would believe them anyway. Vampires are especially good at keeping secrets. Well, most vampires anyway. I'm obviously an exception to the rule occasionally.

"How—? How did you do that?" Jennifer stutters from behind me.

"They're just young punks," I shrug. "If they think they can bully someone, they will. When they get the least bit of opposition from an intimidating man, they run away scared."

"I'm so glad you walked up when you did. You saved my life, and I don't even know your name. Saying thank you is hardly enough."

"My name is Ramses," I reply. "No need to thank me. It was my pleasure."

"How can I ever repay you?" Her tone turns seductive, and she bats her eyelashes playfully. Her thoughts scream of her attraction to me. She quickly makes up her mind that a one-night stand with the man who saved her life will make the perfect story to tell her friends back home. A guilt-free vacation fling that will justify her impulsive actions. Only she's already decided, so it's not exactly an impulsive move. She's simply waiting for my suggestion.

I do hate to disappoint.

"Stay with me tonight," I whisper, my lips

against her ear.

"Do you think I'm the type of girl who sleeps with a man as soon as she meets him?"

"I can promise you this, Jennifer. The last thing you'll want to do, all night long, is sleep."

After that promise, the name of her hotel falls from her lips, and within minutes, we're inside her rented room. With the door locked, she turns to face me with hunger in her eyes. But she doesn't know hunger yet. My fingers weave through her hair and grip the roots tightly as I swing her back to the door. I crush my lips to hers, and my tongue slides into her mouth with fervent need. Her enthusiasm matches mine, and she grinds her hips against the bulge in my pants. Hands fly in every direction as we grope and fumble to remove our clothes. I easily lift her, and she wraps her legs around my waist.

"I can't wait, Ramses. Fuck me now," she demands between kisses.

My hips thrust upward as my arms draw her down onto my cock. I slide inside her wet channel, and her inner walls grip me tightly while I continue to surge into her. I thrust mercilessly and repeatedly, and her body quivers and shakes with the intensity of the orgasm that rolls through her. When she hits the peak of her climax, she tilts her head back and fully exposes her beautiful neck.

My fangs sink deep into her skin, puncture the main artery in her neck, and begin to drain the blood from her body. The added sensation brings me to the edge of passion and pushes me completely over, I continue drinking from her as I succumb to my own orgasm. Her body slumps from the blood loss, and I retract my fangs, just shy of killing her. For a moment, I consider turning her instead, but I ultimately decide otherwise.

Jennifer has to die.

I dispose of her body where she'll never be found. Her eyes still register the shock of the moment. The pallor of her skin leaves no doubt of her state.

Now on to the patronizing thugs who saw my true nature.

I'll drink my fill tonight.

Chapter One

Alea Dunn, September 1789

Today is my birthday and should have been the best seventeenth birthday a young lady could have asked for. It should've been, but it wasn't. At all.

"Alea, come down to the parlor for a moment, please," my mother, Frances, called from the bottom of the stairs.

"Coming," I said as I exited my room.

But I had no idea what I was walking into.

"Alea, you remember Sean, of course," Mother said as soon I entered the parlor. "You two were nearly inseparable as young children whenever we visited the Nasters' estate."

"Of course. It's been a long time. How've you

been, Sean?"

"Very well, Alea. It's so nice to see you again." He stood and kissed my cheek in a friendly gesture. His father, Hugh, sat in the chair next to Sean and sported an oddly wide smile.

"Alea, Sean, have a seat. Hugh and I have some good news for both of you." My father, Clarence, inclined his head toward the vacant chairs.

"I'm sure you're both wondering why we're all gathered here. Clarence and I have discussed matters and have come to a conclusion we believe is beneficial to everyone. Sean and Alea, we're pleased to announce the two of you will be married."

I suddenly couldn't breathe. Surely he was kidding. I waited for the room to erupt in laughter. That never happened.

"This union makes the most sense of any scenario we've discussed. You're perfectly matched as far as families are concerned. Combining our businesses will ensure the financial security of both our houses for many generations to come."

The way Hugh spoke regarding the financial benefits of our marriage made me think he was addressing a room full of investors. He outlined all the ways it made sense, the many ways the companies could be expanded, and how the competition wouldn't stand a chance against us. Or rather, against them.

My eyes drifted to my mother's. Though I kept

my expression neutral so I wouldn't embarrass my parents, the torment I felt inside was crushing. When my mother met my gaze, she knew. I could see it in the way she stiffened then squirmed uncomfortably in her seat. She knew I wasn't happy, but she was powerless to stop the events unfolding before us.

I wanted to run away. I wanted to bolt through the door and never look back.

How selfish was that of me?

"Alea, come walk with me?" Sean asked, bringing me out of my thoughts.

"Of course."

"Look at them. Don't they already make a beautiful couple?" Myra, Sean's mother, cooed from behind us.

The fact that my own mother didn't reply didn't escape me.

One of our servants started to follow us, but my father stopped him. "No need to escort them, Phillip. Sean, Alea, stay on the veranda."

Once we were outside, our mutual discomfort became evident when we each released a long held breath. Our eyes met when Sean took my hand in his before we sat together. He kept his voice low and controlled when he spoke.

"I've known you a long time, Alea. I'd like to think we've always been friends."

"We have, Sean. You are most definitely my friend."

"As your friend, I should tell you I had no idea this was happening. You can probably tell from the conversation this wasn't my plan. I've known you long enough to know marrying me wasn't in your plans either. I thought I should get us both out of there before you passed out." His self-deprecating smile warmed my heart, because my friend was behind it, and the last thing I wanted to do was offend him.

"Sean, you're a wonderful man. I very much don't want to hurt your feelings."

"It doesn't hurt my feelings, Alea. I feel the same way you feel right now. You've always been a good friend to me, and I never want to lose that. The truth is, we don't want to marry each other."

"No. We don't. What do we do?"

"I don't know yet. I'll try to figure something out. Let's just get through the rest of the evening the best we can. Don't give them false hope, but don't let on we're not happy just yet. Think you can do that?"

"Okay. Let's just get through today."

When we walked back in, his parents were smiling widely, obviously convinced we were discussing our perfect union. The smiles my parents sported were closer to pain-filled grimaces than anything. They could read my expression despite my best efforts to hide how I felt. Over dinner, the conversation often drifted to reminiscing over the time we spent together during our childhood. No doubt it was an ongoing effort to remind us how perfectly we fit.

Now that I'm alone in my room, the full weight of the evening hits me. I've been betrothed against my will to a young man whose family standing matches mine in numerous ways. They are successful, know what it means to have money, and know what it takes to make more. On paper and at a quick glance, he's perfect for me and I'm perfect for him. Both of our families are well-off, financially speaking. My father's grandfather started our family business when he was a young man. Sean's great-grandfather did the same.

We socialize in the same circles, so we have a lot of the same friends. Our parents are best friends. Even our grandparents were close friends. All these things in common add up to one thing and one thing alone.

Our families will benefit from our union.

Our fathers will make more money, with a lifetime guarantee of a lucrative partnership.

My family's lineage has been engrained in my very existence since the day I was born. I've always been proud to be a Dunn for a reason.

But today is different.

While Sean is a very nice man, I do not love him. He is not the man I want to spend my life with, plan my wedding with, or go on my dream honeymoon with. And I'm not his first choice either. I'm okay with that because I completely understand how he feels. I also know we're both at the mercy of our families.

I dream of a love that consumes me like a wildfire. One that takes my breath away. One that I know I'd wither up and die without him in my life. I want my heart to flutter and my palms to sweat just from being in his presence. Whoever he is.

I feel like I'm being sacrificed at the altar just to give my father and Sean's father more money than they already have.

I've been sold to the highest bidder.

March 1790

Christmas holiday was spent with the family of my husband-to-be. While we are friends, my affections for him have not grown past that in the least. Father thinks I'm intentionally withholding fondness from Sean, though I've assured him in every way I'm not. What must I do to convince him?

Sean and I took a long walk on his estate grounds late one afternoon. His manservant was always nearby, keeping us well within his sights, but far enough away that we had privacy to speak openly. At this stage of our courting, being completely alone is apparently entirely unheard of. Funny, since Sean and I were friends as small children and were able to play together without the same level of scrutiny.

"Alea, I've tried everything I know to do, but I can't get us out of this marriage. I promise I'll be a good husband to you. I'll provide for you and protect you as expected. I'll do my best never to bring dishonor or shame on you," Sean assured me.

But I wasn't sure what he meant exactly, so I pressed him on his choice of words.

"Sean, what do you mean, exactly? That you will do your best never to bring dishonor or shame on me?"

He was much too quiet for far too long while he considered how he should reply and explain himself. After he confessed what was on his mind, I wished he'd taken more time.

"I have certain needs that you can't fulfill for me. My plan is to discreetly manage my desires outside of our arranged marriage. At some point, we'll be expected to produce an heir to carry on the family name. We'll cross that bridge when our hand is forced. Until then, our union will be mostly friendship and appearances."

He explained himself with such cold, detached descriptions, it was almost as if he was just recounting the latest news to me, but about someone else, someone distant to us.

But it's not—it's about us directly. It's about me, and it's about the rest of my life.

What have I gotten myself into?

For the past three months, Mom has spent every waking minute with Sean's mom, Myra. They've planned every aspect of my wedding—from the color of the bridesmaid dresses, to who will print the invitations, to what we'll have to eat at the reception and the celebration dinner.

I've been dragged along every time so I can spend more time with Sean before our wedding night. He was the normal, nice Sean for the first few weeks. Then he began to change, becoming more and more sullen, withdrawn, and curt with me.

By the end of January, he could no longer hide what his urges and inclinations included. The weeks he had spent with me kept him from his activities and made him very cranky. So he threatened me with bodily harm if I outed him, then took me with him to the secret place where he meets his male lover.

So many thoughts ran through my mind when I realized what was happening. What I'd been brought into without prior warning, without my consent. Men are arrested and sentenced to death every day for what they're doing. Their family names are ruined, their family members are publicly shamed, their possessions are sold at auction, and their wives and children are forced to rely on the kindness of distant relatives to take them in.

I'll admit, at first, I was afraid I'd be arrested

with them for simply knowing what was happening without turning them in. Fourteen prisoners were recently put to death for this very crime—and more are still in jail awaiting their sentences. It scared me more than I can explain. Would I be considered an accomplice for simply having knowledge of it?

By the end of February, the weight of the secret was too much to bear any longer. While Mother and Myra were busy in the parlor—making more wedding plans for me—I left Sean to himself and joined my father in his private study.

I've always been close to my father and can talk to him about anything. I prayed that fact held true as I approached him that evening. My intentions were to persuade him to put a stop to the wedding without putting Sean at risk.

The things he does are definitely against the law, but Sean doesn't deserve to die because of it. If that were to happen, if he were to be found out because of me, I could never live with myself. The other concern I have is more self-centered. If we married and he was found out later in life, I'm not sure I could handle the whispers and condemnation from others. People can be so cruel, and when they think they are righteous and someone else isn't, they have no issue with expressing it. Aside from how they'll treat Sean, I'm sure many will question what is wrong with me and why I wasn't enough for him.

"Father, I need to speak with you. Privately and in confidence, please." My voice was strong and sure despite the flips my stomach turned.

"Of course, sweetheart. Come in and close the door behind you."

"I need your word this will stay between just the two of us. Not even Mother can know. It's very important to me," I stressed as I took a seat across from him.

His expression turned serious as he weighed my request. "Asking me to keep this from your mother is an unusual request, so it must be a very serious topic."

"It's a matter of life and death, Father."

A flash of shock crossed his face before his expression changed to a tentative understanding. It was that moment when I realized my father already may have an idea about the bomb I planned to drop on him.

"You have my word, Alea."

"I need you to stop this wedding to Sean. I can't go through with it. In fact, it's best for our entire family the whole thing is forgotten."

"Why? Be more specific."

As much as I hated to say it aloud and risk exposing Sean, because he is my friend no matter what, I had no other choice. "He's actively engaged in unnatural acts with another man."

"Unnatural acts" is the legal term used by

the courts and is prominently featured in our newspapers, listing each man's name and the circumstances surrounding his arrest. Those two words gave my father the full picture of what we faced, and no further explanation was needed.

"I see," he replied and leaned back in his chair. "You're positive of this?"

"I am. One hundred percent."

"I must confess I've heard rumors about him, concerning this very thing. There hasn't been anything concrete, just rumblings and insinuations. But if this is true, if you're absolutely sure, we must delicately extricate ourselves from this situation. Again, Alea, you're absolutely certain?"

"I've met him, Father. Sean has taken me to their secret meeting place. I've been terrified I'd be arrested by association. I can't do it anymore."

His face flushed red, and his hands curled into fists. "He took you with him?"

"He did, but he didn't want to. His hand was forced with all the wedding planning and pushing us to spend more and more time together. How do we get out of this without hurting either of our family names?"

He took a moment to contemplate my question before coming to an acceptable conclusion. "My business is booming, and I'm expanding it into America now. You and your mother will accompany me on my trip at the end of March. It'll be a good excuse to get you away from this situation. Your mother will be excited about going on a family trip together. We can figure out how best to cancel this arrangement when we've put some distance between our families. Until then, you'll have to keep up the pretense of being engaged to Sean."

"I can do that as long as I know it's not my reality. If I have to stay in America, I can do that, too."

"Let's hope there's no need for such drastic measures. The situation may work itself out while we're gone. Perhaps Sean will seek the company of another young lady to replace you while we're away and completely absolve you of your commitment."

"One can only hope. Though, regardless of how it's accomplished, I don't want any harm to come to Sean or his family. The quieter the better. For all of us."

"I agree wholeheartedly, my dear."

"Thank you, Father. I knew I could count on you to help me. Now I'm especially excited for our voyage, and I can't wait for you to inform Mother we're going with you to America!"

He chuckled at my sudden enthusiasm. "You're a good friend to Sean. He would've been lucky to have you as a wife. But you're exactly right—discretion is best. Now, let's go and tell your mother together."

Myra was visibly upset over the news of

our travel plans, but Mother was so excited she momentarily forgot about planning my nuptials. When she realized Myra's distress, Mother assured her we would be back well in time to pull the remaining tasks together for a grand affair.

For the first time in the last six months, I didn't have to fake my happiness.

Sean's expression was a mixture of relief and worry. His eyes sought mine, and I saw the questions hidden in them.

"I know you will miss me terribly, Sean," I teased playfully. "But trust me when I say, you'll be just fine without me."

He seemed to catch my hidden message and gave me a grateful smile. "Come sit outside with me before Mother and I have to leave."

Seated in the gazebo in my backyard, Sean faced me and held my hand for the sake of the eyes watching our every movement. "We're not getting married, are we?"

"No, Sean, we're not. My father and I are working on a way out of it that results in the least amount of drama for either of us. Regardless, you'll never have to worry about being betrayed by me. I'll never do anything that'll cause you to be harmed."

"You really are my best friend, Alea. And I honestly will miss you. If it comes down to it, you can blame me for our problems and save your own reputation."

"I appreciate the offer, but there's no scenario that doesn't result in some sort of scandal, one way or another, unless we jointly decide we're better as friends and refuse to accept the life our parents have decided we'll have. At least then, our parents will be pitied, and we'll just be their immature, rebellious children."

"That could work." Sean winked. "We'll decide for sure when you get back."

"*If* I come back. I may get to America and decide I'm never coming back here again. Save us both some trouble," I teased.

I haven't spoken to Sean since that day in late February. Mother and I have been so busy preparing for our trip to America, there simply hasn't been time. I think we've packed our entire house just to ensure we have everything we'll need while we're away.

The trip across the Atlantic Ocean is expected to take about twenty-five days. I'm not sure how I'll cope with being out at sea for that long, but I can't wait to get to New York.

Our ship leaves within the hour!

May 1790
We've been in America for a month now, and I absolutely love it here. The thrill of exploring a new land aside, I didn't expect to feel so at home.

Though the culture and the city are much different from London proper, New York is a relatively new and thriving city that has a contagious vibrancy.

Father and Mother have met many new friends and forged new relationships in their business dealings. One of those new people is actually both a friend and business partner. His name is Ramses Barnett, and he is positively handsome. I've developed a major crush on him that's becoming increasingly harder to hide.

He's mature and experienced far past his youthful age of twenty-six years. He and my father met almost instantly when we arrived. Ramses is in the banking business, a profession handed down from generation upon generation of Barnett men. He is working with my father on establishing contracts for our shipping business out of the local ports.

The first time he visited our new home, I almost embarrassed myself because I couldn't stop staring at him. He has thick, wavy brown hair, dark chocolate eyes, and gorgeous full lips. He's much taller than I am, and he's so very strong. He helped Mother move several boxes and a huge trunk without the least bit of strain.

I've noticed him watching me when he doesn't think I'm looking. But I can see him out of the corner of my eye. The way he looks at me, the gleam in his eye, touches me like a physical presence. His desire is palpable and causes a stirring low in my belly. The feeling is so strange and unusual, yet welcome and wanted. It warms me from the inside out to think he is romantically interested in me. Honestly, after not being desired by Sean, it feels good to have a handsome man pay a little attention to me. Not that I think Sean's disinterest was my fault, or that it was a slight against me. I guess I just look at it differently for girls than for boys—it feels a lot like rejection at times.

Tonight, several of Father's business associates were at our house. While they mingled, smoked cigars, and nursed their tumblers of bourbon, I withdrew to my favorite room in the house, the library. The books keep me company, the stories take me on adventures, and the characters are my friends. The door slid open, and there he stood, larger than life and striking in his suit. Though he fit the part of a banker perfectly, he had a wild glint in his eyes as they flicked around the room before settling on mine.

He quickly relaxed his expression before speaking. "I'm sorry if I startled you. I didn't know you were in here."

"It's no problem at all. Do you need the room for a meeting or anything?" I stood, preparing to take my book with me to my bedroom.

"No, nothing like that. In truth, I was looking for you, but I wasn't sure what to say when I found you." In contrast to the confident air he projected, he looked almost shy after his confession.

"You were looking for me?"

He nodded.

"Is there something you need? Something I can get you?" We have house servants to attend to his every need, but it was the only excuse I could think of on the spot. I secretly wanted to give him the chance to confess his undying love for me...or at least his interest in getting to know me better.

He shook his head. "I obviously didn't think this through to completion. My intentions are simply to have a moment alone to talk with you. Do you mind if I sit with you in here for a moment or two?"

"Not at all." Somehow I managed to answer him without making a complete fool of myself.

"We've been formally introduced, but I've never had the pleasure of speaking with you one-on-one. This is somewhat unorthodox, and I realize I'm running the risk of offending your father, but I can't seem to help myself."

"I'm glad you found me. I'm flattered, and I'd also like to spend more time with you. Do you plan to speak to my father about this?"

"I do. But he mentioned in passing that you're to marry a man in England. Did I misunderstand that?"

"Yes and no. It's complicated. The fact is I am engaged in words only. An announcement of our change of heart hasn't been made yet. We'd rather spare both of our families the embarrassment of a mismatched union as long as possible, give people time to move on to bigger and better news first."

"Any man who thinks you're a mismatch for him is a fool. But, selfishly, I'm very glad to hear you're not marrying him."

"He really is a nice man. We've been friends since we were children. It's just not meant to be, and I'm glad my father realizes that. But what about you? What brought you to America?"

"My brother and I run our business together. With the opportunities to expand our enterprise, we couldn't pass it up. So, we crossed the big blue ocean and have been here for quite a while. We like it and have no plans of returning anytime soon."

"Where is your brother? I don't believe I've met him yet."

"He's working with a couple of our other clients. Clarence has kept me very busy with his contracts, so we decided to divide and conquer. I'll be glad to introduce you to him when he's able to join us. Do you have any siblings?"

"No. I'm an only child. From what I understand, my parents wanted to have more children, but my mother had a difficult pregnancy. Neither of them is big on taking unnecessary risks, I'm afraid." I averted my eyes from his, because my entire life had been spent avoiding unnecessary risks, and it was stifling and suffocating.

"A little risk now and then can be so much fun, though. The thrill of getting away with something you never thought you'd do. I have a strong feeling you'd enjoy a little risk-taking." His eyes glimmered with playful mischief, and I found myself smiling and agreeing with him.

Voices carried down the hall, signaling an end to the festivities as our guests moved toward the door. Ramses stood, took my hand in his, and lifted it to his mouth. I watched, mesmerized, as he kissed the back of my hand. His lips were so soft against my skin, but the predatory gleam that held my gaze was unmistakably all-masculine.

"Until tomorrow night, my dear, sweet Alea."

Ramses is coming back over tomorrow night for a celebratory soiree Father has planned for the closure of yet another successful business venture with different guests. Ramses was instrumental in helping to secure it, and Father wants to recognize Ramses as the man of the hour by introducing him to even more influential businessmen. He said this one contract Ramses facilitated is large enough to keep our shipping business busy flowing out of America for the next several years, ensuring a yearly return to America to oversee the holdings.

I'm so excited I get to see him again, I've already planned my entire wardrobe and hairstyle. He's been the perfect gentleman, but I'm concerned he only sees me as a child. I'll be eighteen this year; I'm plenty old enough now, and my plan is to demonstrate that very fact to him tomorrow night.

Chapter Two

Ramses Barnett, 1790

I spent the evening at the same place I've been for the last couple of weeks—the home of Clarence Dunn, a wealthy shipping tycoon who traveled across the Atlantic with his wife and daughter in tow. His business is growing, and he's expanding it to a new continent. His daughter is young and beautiful, and my thirst for her has surpassed being painful and entered the realm of cruelty. The first time I visited their home, I almost turned around and left as soon as I walked through the door. I know myself well enough to recognize the early warning signs of losing control.

However, I stayed and worked on my issue of being too impulsive. I've returned there several times, torturing myself in her presence, and becoming somewhat of a masochist in the process. The more I'm near her, the more my thirst commands me, and the more I'm forced to command it in return. It's strange because the more I control my whims and the more pain I subject myself to, the sweeter my reward will be when I finally have her in my grasp.

Tonight, I tested myself by joining her in the library where she sat completely alone. Though I was able to carry on a completely civil conversation, my eyes continuously strayed to her neck where I could see her jugular vein jumping with every beat of her heart. Kissing her hand good night signaled I'd passed the test, since I didn't sink my teeth into her right then and there. My younger brother is correct when he reminds me our business ventures are more important than my thirst. With prudent investing, the money we make from it will sustain us for a considerable time.

But I passed a girl on the street while walking home tonight I was unable to resist—not physically and not by bloodlust. She was one of the working girls, but there was no denying she was new to the trade. Unlike the others who smelled as if they only bathed once a week, she was fresh and clean. Her long hair was black and shiny, a natural sheen that shimmered in the candlelight. Her corset was too small, forcing her ample cleavage to spill over the top. Her nipples were barely hidden by the lacy fabric, the upper curve of her areolas completely visible. My fangs nearly took on a life of their own as desire coursed through me. And hunger. Deep, physical hunger pangs that urged me to bite into her beautiful skin.

My physical needs didn't end when I became a vampire. My enhanced senses made my sexual desires become even more pronounced and demanding. It had been several weeks since I'd last indulged, but tonight's whim was more than enough to make up for my dry spell. Her name was Richelle, and she was perfect in every way. Her sweet, shy smile. The innocent way she batted her eyes at me. The furtive way she cast sidelong, come-hither glances at me. My cock was hard as steel from the aroma of her arousal alone.

She wasn't acting, putting on a show to earn money. Her attraction to me was genuine, and that excited me more than anything.

"Hello, beautiful." I approached her as a gentleman would, not giving away I knew she was a prostitute. Making the game a little more interesting.

"Hello, yourself," she purred. "Are you alone tonight? A handsome young man like yourself?"

"I am, actually. I haven't found that special lady to spend my life with yet."

"Maybe you should try one night instead of a whole lifetime," she offered suggestively.

"Does that mean you're free tonight?"

"I'm available, but I'm not free." Her coy smile left no doubt of her meaning. And I had no doubt I'd take her up on her very tempting offer.

"I would say the pleasure would be all mine, but that would be a lie. You will thoroughly enjoy a night with me. Shall we?" I extended my hand to take hers, and she slipped her small hand into mine willingly.

"I'm all yours. Where to?"

"It's only a few blocks to my brownstone. Let's take a walk."

We chatted on the short walk to my place about everything and nothing special. She said she's an orphan after both her parents fell ill with yellow fever. As she walked and talked, I couldn't take my eyes off her breasts and the way they bounced. She was oblivious to it, or perhaps she was accustomed to the way men stared at her. As we passed a darkened alleyway, I pushed her into it and held her against the brick wall.

To calm her frightened response, because I was nowhere near ready to be done with her, I smiled warmly. "I just need a taste of you before we get to my place. Watching you walk is too much for me to resist. Just a little nip."

She didn't catch the double entendre of my words. But it was no matter. She relaxed just the same and wordlessly offered her body for my taking.

A slight tug on the top of her corset freed her breast, and I quickly covered her taut nipple with my mouth. I sucked on the sensitive peak, changing pressure from hard to soft without warning. My teeth grazed over the edge before I pulled more of her flesh into my mouth again. I kneaded her breast with one hand, while holding both of her hands above her head with the other. I had to consciously remind myself not to get carried away and accidently hurt her with my innate strength.

"Mmm," she moaned. "You're so good at that. I knew you would be a wonderful lover by just looking at you."

"And tasting you like this only makes me want more. Come, my dear, let's see if we can make it all the way to my place without stopping again."

She began to stuff her ample breast back into her corset, but I stopped her with a gentle touch of my hand. "Leave it out. I'll make sure it's covered for you."

She eyed me suspiciously, but she did as I asked anyway. I pulled her to my side and draped my arm over her shoulder. She was so small, especially compared to me, I had no problem hiding her exposure by sliding my hand over it. The intimate gesture made her giggle, and the sound of her laughter mixed with the weight of her breast in my hand shot electric surges straight to my cock.

"Turn into me slightly and put your hand on my

cock, Richelle."

She did as I asked without question, and she gasped when she felt the thick bulge in my pants. "It's so big." Her small fingers traced the outline of me to test the full size and girth I had to offer. "I'm glad it's already late. I'm sure I couldn't handle another customer after you tonight."

"No, Richelle, I can guarantee you won't have another customer after I'm done with you for the night."

I opened the door of my brownstone and let her enter first. Her eyes roamed around, taking in all my fine décor, and uncertainty settled in her eyes. "Sir, you have a fine home. It's not my place to say, but you should have a wife to take care of your needs. Not someone like me."

"You are exactly what I need to take care of my needs, Richelle. You can call me Ramses. It's a name you'll be screaming in pleasure very soon."

Her eyes flitted down to my crotch, and she licked her lips. "I have no doubt of that. Where do you want me first?"

"Take off your clothes and bend over the back of the settee," I commanded without hesitation.

She complied without reluctance. It was beautiful. The perfectly round globes of her ass called to me, and I planned to have her in every way imaginable. But first, the glistening folds of her already wet pussy needed attention. I shed my clothes in a split second and gripped her hips from behind.

"Hold on tight. I'm going to fuck you tonight until you're my personal rag doll. But my intentions are not to hurt you, so tell me if I'm too rough. Otherwise, I'll assume your screams mean you want more."

"I can hardly wait as it is. I'm ready, Ramses."

Though she couldn't see me, I smiled at her reply. *She's ready, is she?* My engorged cock said we were more than ready. I positioned myself at her entrance and slid the head of my dick up and down her soaked slit. Coated with her desire as a lubricant, I thrust my hips forward and drove into her to the hilt. She cried out in a mixture of pain and pleasure, unable to distinguish one from the other. She adjusted her stance, widening her legs, and began to move back and forth along my shaft of her own accord.

I guessed that meant she wanted more. And I was all too happy to oblige her.

She met my thrusts, pound for pound, and my fingers dug into her skin and held her hip bones in my grip. The ripples from her repeated orgasms gripped my length like fingers, tightly holding on and heating me to the core. I leaned over, my chest flat against her back, and slid my hand around to her clit. With the change in angle and the additional pressure on the bundle of pleasure sensors, her screams echoed off the walls around us.

My fangs slid out, ready to bite the back of her neck, but I reined them in. It was much too soon to stop fucking her. She felt too good with her tight little cunt wrapped around my thick cock. The scent of her arousal that filled the room was too intoxicating. And I had so much more energy to expend before we ended the night. Instead of using my fangs, I left my mark on her smooth skin with my teeth.

After moving around to the padded seat of the settee, I laid her on her back and resumed making good on my rag doll promise. Her breasts, free from the constraints of the corset, bounced in cadence with my thrusts. I slid my hands up, gripped her breasts, and held on as she reached the pinnacle of pleasure once again.

"This will be mine tonight, too." I slid my finger in her ass, and she dug her fingernails into my skin. With every thrust of my hips, my finger pushed deeper inside her puckered rosebud. When a wave of wetness coated my cock, I knew her body welcomed the foreign intrusion, and I added a second finger. "You like that, don't you?" She moaned in pleasure, her wetness running down and coating my fingers. Her own fluids provided the perfect lubricant as I continued stretching her.

"Fuck, you feel incredible," she panted. "I love how you fuck me."

Her crude language was unheard of in the prim and proper circles my brother and I normally associated with. It turned me on and fueled my carnal desires even more than usual. I drove into her harder, still using only a small fraction of the power I possessed, but her human body wouldn't be able to handle me at full force. It only took a few more seconds before her entire body shuddered as her climax tore through her.

"Oh my God, Ramses!" she screamed with her release.

The second I felt all her internal muscles relax, I withdrew from her sweet pussy and pushed into her tight little ass. Still high on her last orgasm, her body more easily accepted my drenched cock, though I took extra care not to intentionally cause harm. Her face instantly contorted in pain from the stretching burn of her delicate tissues. Plunging my fingers in her pussy brought her the pleasure she needed to relax again and allowed me to resume my tandem assault of pleasure on her body. Before long, her muscles once again tensed, but that time, from decadent hedonism. The tight muscle in her ass clamped down around my cock as she came and forced us both over the edge into pure bliss.

"Don't plan on leaving tonight, Richelle. I'm hardly finished with you." My voice left no room for argument, and the sated expression on her face showed no contention.

"I'm not going anywhere. I just need a nap first, if that's all right. You've worn me out like no other man I've ever known."

"I'll take you to my bed. You'll be more comfortable there. Sleep while you can. When I wake you, it'll be with my cock in your mouth."

"That's sure to give me sweet dreams, Ramses."

Her response shocked me, and I've never been easy to surprise. The smile that crawled across her face was tantalizing and enticing—she liked the imagery my words created in her mind.

I picked her up off the settee, and she wrapped her arms around my neck, snuggling her face in close to me. I carried her to my bedroom and deposited her on my bed before I decided to make good on my promise right there, before she'd had time to recover. It was at that moment I had the most perfect idea, and I once again found myself stunned because it had never occurred to me before now. Before I had this young, beautiful whore in my arms.

She wouldn't die after all, at least, not as a victim of my thirst.

But she would die soon, nonetheless.

She'd die a human death, and then join me as I built our vampire clan.

In my washroom as I cleaned up, I reminisced of how it had been only my brother Slade and me for far too long. It was time to start turning humans into vampires and add more to our little family. I decided right then that Richelle would be the first human in America I'd change. But first I'd need to speak to Slade about my idea. I knew I could keep her in my secluded basement until my brother and I reached an agreement on the size and nature of our clan. She was much too delicious to leave her to chance on the streets.

After all, some madman could get to her out there... One besides me, anyway.

The more I thought about the idea of a large clan, the more I knew it was the right path. We'd have an entire network of vampires with different skills, abilities, and gifts. We'd have to keep it quiet for as long as possible to keep the news from traveling to our old contacts in London before we were ready to face them head on. Watching my little slut as she slept in my bed gave me all sorts of ideas. Vampire brothels, saloons that served both alcohol and human blood, secret business alliances—the possibilities were endless.

First, I needed a taste of her blood. The scent of it still had me close to a frenzied state, and she was sleeping so soundly she'd never know I'd taken a sample. Her bare breast taunted and teased me, so I bent at the waist and pulled her sweet-scented skin into my mouth. She barely stirred. When my fangs slid out and pierced her skin like a quick dart, she jumped and her hand flew to my head. But her eyes never opened because my saliva quickly dulled the pain like a natural anesthetic.

Her blood tasted even better than it smelled.

I showed more self-restraint than I ever realized I possessed.

My mind was made up. Any opposition from Slade be damned.

Coming to America was the best decision of our immortal lives. My brother and I had had quite the windfall of new business ventures, lucrative payouts, and more privacy than we'd ever imagined for the throats that we drained dry.

Chapter Three

Alea Dunn, May 1790

Ramses returned tonight, just as he promised he would. Since the contract that had just been brokered was so significant, Mother had arranged a special sit-down dinner, but she'd transformed the backyard to host hors d'oeuvres and drinks first. She insisted the atmosphere was superior to encourage everyone to mingle. I was inclined to agree with her. With people milling about, talking, eating, and drinking, the chances of my being seen hovering around Ramses were greatly diminished.

As our guests began to arrive, the staff showed them through the patio doors to our late spring oasis. The night air was warm enough a shawl wasn't needed, though I had one picked out that was an exact match for the hue of my crimson dress.

Speaking of, my dress...was...spectacular.

The clothing style in America has proven to be so vastly different from London, I didn't appreciate it at first glance. However, one day while Mother and I window-shopped, the featured dress caught my attention. With its straight lines and understated elegance, I simply couldn't resist purchasing it. The front has a deeply scooped chest, reminiscent of Marie Antoinette's style, but the sleeves are short and barely cover the tops of my shoulders. The waistline is high with a sash that ties in the back. The sash combined with the low neckline accentuates my breasts and makes me feel very grown-up. The bottom is flowing and so very romantic, unlike the stuffy, formal hoop dresses I grew up wearing.

I've normally stayed far away from Father's business gatherings because the dull conversation nearly bores me into a coma. The thick smoke from the cigars makes me cough, and the sweet stench of the tobacco turns my stomach. Tonight was the first time I've joined any business dinner willingly and without being asked first. But then, I've never really had a reason to want to go before Mr. Ramses Barnett arrived on the scene.

I made my entrance after everyone had arrived and settled into their comfortable conversation routine. As I stepped onto the lanai, the warm breeze greeted me, blowing my long blond hair away from my face. I rarely wear it down with the ends curled as it is tonight, but I chose that style because it makes me look older, more mature. More sophisticated. More worldly.

And then Ramses looked up at me. For the first time in my life, I felt desired. Wanted. *Needed*—in the same way someone drowning needs a breath of air. In the same way a man dying of thirst needs water. In the same way a sick person needs health. In the same way someone starving needs a bite to eat.

With that one look from him, everything else faded to black in the background. All I could see was him. All I could hear was my heart thumping in my chest. While the small band played their original music for the other guests, the erratic beat of my heart rivaled them by creating its own music.

Ramses approached me and held his hand out after he bowed slightly. I accepted his hand, and he pulled me closer to him in a partner dance. With one hand on my waist and the other holding my hand in the air, he led us around the dance floor with grace and ease. I don't think I moved my eyes away from his penetrating stare even once during the entire song.

"Alea, have you found a way to let that poor sap down so you're not officially engaged anymore?"

"Since last night?" I laughed, and he flashed his most charming smile.

"I guess I'd hoped your father would send a letter first thing this morning."

"Sean is my friend, nothing more. No matter what, I wouldn't wish anything bad to happen to him."

"Why would anything bad happen to him?"

"You know how people are," I hedged. "If they think there's anything to talk about, they'll blow it all out of proportion with rumors. We just want to head that off at the pass as much as we can."

"That's very honorable. On top of being so beautiful and intelligent, you're also thoughtful and considerate. There are so many things to love about you, Alea."

His directness is so new to me, especially with what he said last night. He doesn't seem like a young man freshly arrived here from London's high society. But then again, I've never really been around other men his age. Only Father's business associates, and that's exactly why I stayed away from their meetings as much as possible. Ramses is actually quite refreshing and doesn't leave me guessing what he's thinking.

"I'm surprised you haven't already found a nice lady to settle down with and have a family." The words flew out of my mouth before I could stop them. I've never said anything so rude in my life, and I thought I'd die of embarrassment on the spot.

"It's not for a lack of a few ladies trying to

capture that spot. Or for my mother to fill it, when she was still alive. But I guess I just haven't found the right one. Up until now, at least."

His words flew straight to my already overactive heart. Could he really mean that? Is he falling in love with me? The possibility of it being true, that he'd actually choose me, fills me with such excitement. After our dance, we sat together at a small table outside, enjoying a glass of champagne and each other's company. Ramses is so witty and knowledgeable in so many things, I could never grow tired of talking to him, listening to him.

I waited until everyone left and retired to my bedroom to capture every word floating in my memory about tonight, so I'd never forget a single thing. How wonderful it felt to be in his arms. How captivating his eyes are. How he seems to see straight through me and somehow knows exactly what I'm thinking and feeling before I even say a word. How he hangs on every word I say, like it's the most important matter in the world. All through dinner, our eyes found each other and further sealed our bond.

Father just called me down to his study to discuss the events of the night. My tears are falling so fast now, I'm not sure how this ink will even dry on the page. He noticed the connection between Ramses and me, and he's not happy.

"Alea, it's obvious you're very smitten with

Ramses Barnett. Actually, it's a little too obvious for my taste. When he visits our home, it's for my business. He's an associate of mine, and I won't have your schoolgirl crush interfere with my plans. The fact is, I have a very strong feeling about him. Call it gut instinct. But I won't allow him to use my daughter's infatuation with him against me in our negotiations.

"The next time he visits, I expect you to be on your best, proper behavior. If you can't control yourself around him, you'll have to dine alone in your room and wait until our guests have left before coming down to join your mother and me. You are not yet eighteen. You are still betrothed to a man in England. Some of our guests will travel back home before we do, and they'll talk, Alea. There is simply too much at stake for you to behave so foolishly. Have I made myself perfectly clear?"

By the time Father finished speaking, his voice had risen several levels. I can't remember a time he's ever yelled at me before. But what he yelled at me about both hurt and embarrassed me. It hurt because he essentially banned me from being around Ramses, or at least, from showing my interest in him. Which just comes out naturally when I'm around him. It's not a conscious decision—he just makes me feel so real. I was also hurt because he's right. I am making a fool of myself. Ramses could be just using me to gain leverage over my father's business deals.

But most of all, someone could go back and tell others about my behavior, putting unnecessary attention on Sean, when that's the very thing we're trying to avoid. He's my friend, and his well-being never even crossed my mind. If Sean is hurt because of my carelessness, I don't know what I'll do.

I'm embarrassed because my behavior is obviously overly blatant and deeply inappropriate. My parents are ashamed of my unseemly flirting with Ramses, who's a slightly older man, considering he's twenty-six and I'm still seventeen. Father's business associates also witnessed it, and they will think the same about me. What if they accuse my father of giving Ramses preferential treatment because of me? What if all of this harms his business?

I've been so very foolish and thought only of myself. It's pathetic, really, now that a mirror has been put in front of my face. With that, I simply can't face Ramses or the others tomorrow when they come to our house again. Not tomorrow night. Maybe not even the next night. The tongue-lashing I received is much worse than just disappointing my father. I'm disappointed in myself.

Ramses Barnett, 1790
Young, inexperienced girls are so easy to persuade. Their opinions aren't firm, so they're

very easy to coax and sway in the direction I need them to go. Especially with the added benefit of reading their thoughts. Of knowing exactly what to do, when to do it, and how far to push them past where they've always been comfortable going before. With Miss Alea Dunn, I don't even have to use my vampire powers to know what she's thinking. It's written all over her face, in the blush of her skin, and in the bat of her soft brown eyes. She wants me almost as much as I want her. Well, her blood, anyway. There's no doubt I'll enjoy her body and take her virginity first.

Knowing she's never been touched is more of a turn-on for me than I ever would've imagined. Being the first to show her *everything* would make me her master every bit as much as turning her would. The problem is, I don't know if I can turn her. I don't know if I can stop drinking her blood once I start. I've always lacked a measure of self-control when certain humans have been involved. But I've never experienced anything near the need I have to consume her—completely, utterly, thoroughly drain every last drop from her veins. It's the only reason I keep returning to her family's stuffy affairs.

After the last gathering at the Dunn's several days ago, Slade and I had the first significant fight we've had in decades. My brother knows me too well and can read me inside and out. He has always watched my mood swings closely. Even I have to admit he's had cause to be troubled over my actions in the past. But I won't admit that to him—ever. He's the younger one, but he has had to be the voice of reason on more than one occasion. He had to be because I couldn't.

"Ramses, you are playing a dangerous game yet again. Stop this right now before you go too far. Once you've crossed that line, you know there's no turning back. There is too much at stake, and I *will not* let you ruin this good thing we have here. If I have to, I'll stop you myself." Slade's tone was all too familiar—he was at his wit's end with me. He'd never threatened me before, but I had absolutely no doubt he meant exactly what he said.

"Slade, I need you to trust me."

"You haven't given me much reason to trust you. Your past record speaks for itself."

There may have been a couple of times during my vampiric life my craving became a full obsession that consumed me. I would've gone to the ends of the world and back just to satisfy that urge. That need. That yearning. It's so deep inside me, it permeates every dead cell and fiber in my body and takes over any rational thinking I otherwise possess. Those... episodes...are far behind me now. That's not what's happening to me with this girl. It feels different.

"I'm fine, Slade. Stop worrying so much."

"Your infatuation with this Dunn girl gives me plenty of cause to worry. I've seen the crazed look in your eye when you get back from the meetings at her house. I know that look far too well, and I know what comes afterward. End this tonight, Ramses." He shoved me and knocked me a few steps backward to drive his point home. My brother's strength has surpassed my own, both physically and mentally, through his focus and determination. He could use his telepathic power to force me to obey him if he wanted, but he was never that type of man, and his code of honor stayed with him through his change.

It's true, I cannot deny how often I think about the scent of her blood and how exquisite it would be to feast on her. Once I started, I know I wouldn't be able to stop. I wouldn't be able to get enough of her, until there was none of her left. Slade's concern is that by killing her, I'll fall into a depressive state, take my vengeance out on too many others, and then we'd be discovered.

"I can't just walk away from this, Slade. We're making a fortune from Clarence Dunn, and there are more contracts to finalize," I bellowed back at him.

"Then I will finish it. You are not to go back to that house again. Or you will regret it."

But I have an amazing plan this time that will keep my mind on track.

I am going back to that house.

I will have every last drop of Alea's blood.

Slade will see my reasoning, the purpose of my

plan.

He left after our outburst, and I returned to my secret place, where my sweet Richelle waited for me. The first night, she was too worn out from our bedroom antics and slept all night. It wasn't until the following day that she realized she was my permanent guest. Her initial reaction was pure disbelief. She thought I was joking, playing with her, only wanting to keep her as my sex slave. When she realized she belonged to me, intense fear and instant pleading for her release followed. After I'd left her alone for several hours, she was raging mad when I returned.

Her rage only served to stoke the fires of my libido, and I made the most of it. I'm pleased to say I fucked her into submission. She feels safer now, back to the original thought that she's simply my sex slave. She actually likes it because I take good care of her, so she's accepted her fate. I haven't changed her yet, though I have enjoyed tastes of her blood without her fully realizing what happened. She has questioned some of the puncture marks and playfully accused me of having a fetish for biting.

She has no idea.

But she soon will.

Chapter Four

Alea Dunn, June 1790

I've done as Father said and stayed away from his work dinners and social events over the past month. It has killed me to know Ramses has been downstairs, but I couldn't go down to see him. He has been so close, but he may as well have been across the ocean for all the good it has done me.

I've watched through the window when no one was looking. They were all too busy with their drinks, food, and conversation to notice me anyway. I've been ordered to stay inside, like a little child ordered to play in my room and not bother the adults. Even if I were invited to join them now, I'd be much too embarrassed to show my face.

But that doesn't stop me from watching from the cover of darkness in my room. In the spare bedrooms upstairs. From any window that gives me a good view of Ramses. Sometimes I wish he'd see me, scale the wall outside, and whisk me away with him. But that is the wish of a child, of a young girl who still believes in fairy tales. Wishing for a fairy-tale ending is a luxury I can no longer afford.

"They found another body?" I asked Mother when I picked up the newspaper from the table. The morning's paper showed the fourth dead body was found within the last three weeks. "Is there a madman lose from an asylum somewhere?"

She tried to hide her worried expression with her nonchalant tone. "People die every day for many different reasons, Alea. There's no need to be so dramatic about it. Just because a body was found doesn't mean someone killed them. They very well could've died a natural death."

"Mother, at some point you'll have to accept the fact that I'm grown now. In a short few months, I'll be eighteen. Stop shielding me from the world—I have to live in it."

Her eyes flew up to meet mine, and she really looked at me for what felt like the first time in a very long time. "I suppose you're right, Alea. You are growing up, too fast for my taste, but it's happening whether I like it or not. The bodies of four girls have been found recently. What the papers aren't printing is the manner in which their bodies were found. There must be a madman out there, with what's been done to those poor souls."

I'd never heard Mother sound so frightened before. I could only imagine what they'd talked about while I wasn't part of the adult conversation. Still, she was nervous and didn't exactly want to discuss it. But I pushed, because I could tell she knew more than what she'd already said.

"What does he do to them?" My voice came out as a whisper.

She pursed her lips together, forming a thin line and further accentuating her worried expression. She hesitated for just a moment. It didn't feel like she was trying to hide anything from me now. She just simply didn't want to talk about it. "He mutilates them, Alea, in the most aberrant ways. It's worse than what a madman would do. It's like a mindless animal got to them. But an animal wouldn't leave the rest of their bodies. Their throats were ripped out, but there was hardly any blood on them."

My responding gasp was loud and escaped before I could stop it. My hands flew over my mouth when I pictured their bodies, torn apart and lifeless. "Who could do such a thing?"

"No one knows, Alea. Everyone is taking extra precautions when they go out at night now. I guess the only consolation is all the dead girls were prostitutes, so maybe he's not targeting anyone else. But we can't assume that's the case. I just hope and pray they find this murderer soon so we can put this whole terrifying ordeal behind us."

I read the article in the paper while having breakfast, and I've never had a heavier heart. Those poor girls didn't deserve to die like that. How frightened they must have been. How much pain they must have experienced at the killer's hand. And the killer, what of him? What sort of madness flows through his veins and makes him want to do such vile things?

"Alea, we have to go to the tailor's shop today. Eat your food and get dressed. I'd like to be finished there as early as possible. It's a short walk from here, and the weather is so nice, but I don't want to be out anywhere close to dark."

The way she alternated between wringing her hands and wiping them on her dress told me more than I wanted to know. My stomach was on edge after reading the newspaper anyway, so I left my breakfast half-eaten and dressed as quickly as possible. Mother and I left the house, walking and chatting about nothing important. Anything that might keep our thoughts from straying too much.

But it didn't work.

What Mother didn't tell me, and what the newspaper didn't mention, was how many family members were walking the sidewalks with panic-stricken expressions. They approached anyone they passed, showed drawings of their missing loved ones, and asked if anyone had seen them. One mother thrust the drawing at me, startling me with her forwardness.

"Child, have you seen this girl anywhere? She's my daughter. My sweet, young daughter. Is she your friend, by any chance?" Her cheeks were tear-stained, her eyes were bloodshot, and her face was gaunt. It appeared she hadn't eaten in days, and I wondered if she'd been out there looking for her daughter all that time without any food.

"No, I'm sorry, ma'am. I don't know her, and I haven't seen her. If I do, I will tell her to go home right away."

It was the most comfort I had to offer her. In the short time I'd been in America, I hadn't made friends with anyone my age. That was a sad fact when I thought about it, but I soon moved on to a different thought when the next person asked if I'd seen her missing son. As I looked around the crowded streets, I saw several more people with sketches. One thing they all had in common was they all appeared to be poor—in dress, in conduct, in status.

"Mother, do you see what I see?"

"What do you mean?"

"The murdered girls, they were all prostitutes. All these missing people, they're all poor. He's picking people he thinks won't be missed. He probably didn't think all these people would be out searching for them."

"You think these missing people are also his victims?"

"It would make sense, wouldn't it? Have you ever seen this many people out, desperate to find their missing family members? There are too many for this to be a coincidence. It's scary, Mother. If he'd do all this, what else is he capable of doing?"

"I hope we never find out, my girl. Here we are." She motioned for me to enter the door on my right, into the seamstress shop. "We've been invited to a ball, and we need proper gowns to wear. We'll have beautiful brand-new ones made for it."

"You mean I'm going with you?"

"Yes, Alea, you're going to the ball, too. I've spoken with your father and convinced him you can act like a mature lady long enough to go with us. The ball will be held in six weeks. We barely have time to have one suitable gown made, much less two, but this seamstress comes highly recommended. Do not disappoint me." Her tone and her eyes held the warning that needed no further explanation.

Stay away from Ramses Barnett.

Ramses Barnett, 1790

I've heard Alea's thoughts loud and clear every time I've visited the Dunn residence. She watches from the windows, wishing she could join us, angry she's treated like a child. When she finds me in the crowd, her notions take a drastic turn. Visions of her and me in various stages of a sensual dance replay in her mind.

If she only knew how much further I could take her fantasies, how much I could teach her, and how much she'd love every second of it. She's young, inexperienced, and is prone to fantasy. What she doesn't know yet is reality is so much more pleasurable and satisfying. Her passion is so strong at times I can feel it radiating from her thoughts. One more thing to throw fuel on my own fire.

Slade has been so busy with his own clients, he hasn't paid much attention to me and what I've been doing since the fight we had. Which is a good thing, because I've been very busy. After leaving the Dunns', I've gone out on hunting sprees and enjoyed the spoils of the night. It's way too easy to prey on humans. They're gullible, trusting, and think everyone is inherently good. But I've been a very bad boy. If Slade ever noticed my absence, my plan was to tell him I'd been in the forest, relieving my insatiable thirst.

"Hello, beautiful. Do you live around here?" I delivered my line flawlessly, feigning concern for the current victim's well-being. She was beautiful and young. With her flowing red hair in long, loose curls, her porcelain complexion, and her toned body, she was the epitome of gorgeous.

I had a desperate need to add her to my collection.

"Only a few blocks north of here, actually. Do I know you?" She narrowed her eyes and studied my face, like she was sure she'd seen me before but couldn't place where.

"No, ma'am," I replied cordially. "I'm positive I would remember you if we'd met before. My name is Ramses. And you are?"

She smiled and dropped her eyes to the ground in modesty. The pink tinge of her cheeks spread down her neck right before my eyes. "You flatter me, sir. I'm Corinne."

"Miss Corinne, I'd be honored if you'd allow me to walk you home. A lovely lady such as yourself should have a gentleman to escort you and make sure you get home safely."

"That's very kind of you, Ramses." Her tone was gracious as she looped her arm with mine.

We were about a block from her house when the crowds thinned out to virtually no one. No witnesses. No one to hear her cries for help. No one to come running if she screamed. It was a nice, quiet neighborhood that hadn't built up as quickly as other parts of the city. In less time than it took to blink, she was in my arms, and we flew through the air to my secret love nest where Richelle waited.

Corinne was understandably confused when we

landed. Moments ago, she was close to her home. Before she realized what had happened, she had no idea where she was. Or who she was with, or what I planned to do with her. But she knew it couldn't be good. She knew she wouldn't be able to escape from my hold. I didn't really have to read her mind to know what she was thinking—I could smell her fear emanating from every pore in her body.

"Sweetheart, just relax. You're breathing too fast. You'll pass out if you don't slow down. You don't want to do that and miss all the fun."

I placed a gentle hand on her shoulder to guide her down the stairs and into the darkened basement. With my strength, she couldn't have walked away from me even if she had her wits about her to do so. The slightest touch was all it took to control her slight body. Too much pressure would crush her bones, but that's not what I wanted for her.

My eyes immediately adjusted to the darkness. Even though I can walk freely in the light, the darkness is my home. I can see better in the pitch black of night than in the bright sunlight. Just one of the advantages of being a vampire. It took Corinne's eyes several minutes longer to adjust enough to make out shapes in the dark. The shapes began to morph into identifiable forms, and she whimpered loudly when realization set in.

First, Corinne saw Richelle stretched out on the bed, naked but partially covered with a sheet.

Corinne's eyes drifted to a couple of small puncture wounds on Richelle's exposed breasts that were almost healed. Her gaze continued along the lines of Richelle's body until she saw the shackle around Richelle's ankle, then along the chain to where it was attached to the wall. It was then Corinne knew her fate had been sealed. She knew I'd never let her leave and risk being discovered. She knew, without a shadow of a doubt, she was mine.

"Corinne, this is Richelle. You'll be keeping her company for a while. You're both here for my pleasure. But my pleasure will definitely also be your pleasure. Come. Let me show you."

Her dress ripped completely in two with a quick tug on the back and crumpled to the floor in a pile at her feet. Her hands flew up to cover her breasts, and I just smiled to myself. A similar pull on her panties left them in shreds, and she was out of hands to cover all her best parts. While still standing behind her, I laid my hands on her shoulders and gently caressed the skin down her arms, straightening them at her sides as I moved.

My hands slid around her waist, reveling in the softness of her skin, and glided up her taut stomach to cup each breast in my hand. My cock had already stiffened from the scent of her fear, her blood, and her pussy combined. When I squeezed her nipple between my thumb and index finger, she tried to hold in her sigh of pleasure, but I heard it just the same. I leaned in and put my mouth close to her ear.

"Corinne, relax. Stop worrying. I'll make you feel so good, you'll be sorry you didn't meet me sooner."

Her perky, round breast was a perfect fit for my hand and was too enticing to let go. As I continued to squeeze it and tease the rigid peak of her nipple, my other hand slid down the center of her body to the tight curls that covered her pussy. "If my fingers were to find their way inside that sweet, tight pussy of yours, would it already be wet? Would I find that you want me as much as I want you?"

With only a soft touch, my fingers lightly grazed back and forth across her several times, barely giving her a sense of what she'd been missing. Within seconds, her body responded as I knew it would, and her head fell back against my shoulder. When her stance widened slightly, I knew she was more than ready. She was practically begging for more, for the release her body demanded.

"Mmm, you do," I murmured in her ear as my fingers pushed into her pussy. "You're so wet, but you're still so tight. You almost take my self-control away completely. It's all I can do to take it slow and not fuck your little pussy into tomorrow."

Her head lolled to the side as my fingers continued to pump in and out of her wetness. The temptation was too much to resist. When the first orgasm tore through her body, her pussy clenched around my fingers, and my fangs sank into her skin. Just a small taste of her was all I needed. That's what I told myself, anyway.

After I laid her down on the bed next to Richelle, Corinne watched spellbound as I shed my clothes and removed Richelle's shackle. Richelle licked her lips when my cock sprang free, and I agreed she had a brilliant idea. "Take me in your mouth, Corinne."

She obeyed my command and wrapped her beautiful, pink lips around the head of my cock. Her tongue rolled around it before she took me all the way in, and I felt the back of her throat against the tip of my dick. The warmth and wetness of her soft mouth surrounded me, and my hips moved back and forth without conscious thought. Richelle squirmed next to us, aching to join. I extended one arm and thrust my fingers into Richelle's eager pussy and kept one on Corinne's head while she continued to suck my dick.

After I adjusted our positions, Richelle straddled my face while I feasted on her sweetness, and Corinne kept working her talented mouth up and down my shaft. My tongue circled and grazed Richelle's clit as my fingers plunged deep inside her, curling to hit the spot that made her scream. My hips continued to buck on their own, fucking Corinne's mouth with each glide of her tongue.

"Climb on top and fuck me, Corinne."

She straddled my hips, positioned the tip of my cock at her wet entrance, and slid down on me until I disappeared inside her. I felt the small pop inside her, and I knew I was the first to venture into her uncharted territory. She was well under my trance, not feeling any pain, but she would be sore the next morning. For that moment, though, she was erotically mine. Like a professional, she rode me like she owned me, like she'd been created just to satisfy my carnal needs. Her tight little pussy gripped and contracted around me, squeezing me with her velvety inner fingers, extracting every bit of me when she tumbled over her own peak.

"What about me?" Richelle asked with a slight pout.

"There's plenty left for you, sweetheart," I assured her and rearranged our bodies once again.

Standing at the side of the bed with Richelle pulled to the very edge, I entered her with one swift thrust and fucked her until I was sure her screams would wake the dead. Their bodies spent and as limp as rag dolls, I crawled into the bed between them, and they curled into my sides and slept with their heads in the crooks of my shoulders, my arms cradling them.

I knew I'd have to leave them soon to go feed. While I was out, I planned to look for more humans to add to my clan. Richelle and Corinne satisfied my needs for the moment, staying my fangs from devouring Alea, but they were only a momentary distraction. That distraction would only last for so long, especially when Alea consumed more and more of my thoughts.

The dark mood began to infiltrate my mind again, regardless of how hard I tried to hold it off. It originated from my inability to have what I craved the most. Alea. The two substitutes in my bed would only work for so long before I snapped. The darkness that shrouded my mind sometimes completely took me over, and I didn't always remember what I did when I was under its influence.

Even as strong as I was, I knew it was only a matter of time.

What I didn't know was time was about to be up.

Though I could read minds, I couldn't see the future.

Chapter Five

Slade Barnett, July 1790

I have to keep reminding myself how much I love my brother. Over and over, I have to chant that fact in my mind to keep from tracking him down and wringing his neck. Yesterday, a visitor stopped by my office because he hasn't been able to find Ramses for the last few days, and a crucial meeting is coming up with a major client. A man who has brought more money to us than any other single person.

And Ramses is in the midst of one of his *episodes*.

Dead bodies have been turning up over the last several weeks. Though he denied he was on the verge of another incident, I have no doubt he's behind it.

"I should have fucking known. How the fuck did I miss all the signs?" I bellowed to no one in particular, unable to contain my anger. "Fucking Ramses has fucking done it again. If I get my hands on him, I'll kill him myself!"

"Slade, he's been gone for three weeks now. Clarence has asked multiple times if the upcoming shipping contract has been secured yet. He's becoming very nervous about Ramses's absence and my continued excuses for him. How long did you tell him to stay gone?" Thomas asked.

Thomas Vale is our right-hand man and the best employee we've ever had. He's also the only other one of our business staff who knows my true nature since he's a vampire himself.

"All I told him was to go deep into the forest and fulfill his thirst. The last time we went through one of his insatiable thirst periods, he almost got us both killed. He wasn't discreet in any way—in the people he chose, in how he disposed of the bodies, in how many he killed. He left a trail that led straight back to us, and we narrowly escaped before the town full of pitchfork-wielding citizens had our heads."

"If he's in the forest, we should be safe."

"I don't think he's in the forest. I think he's doing it again. The dead bodies that have turned up recently, the many people who are missing—I think he's behind it all. How long before we're at risk again?"

"Let me do some checking around about him and see what I can find out. In the meantime, you should contact Mr. Dunn just in case you have to finish the last-minute details for Ramses."

I retrieved the client's file from Ramses's office and spent the morning reviewing every detail of the contract and the draft shipping manifest so I could oversee the remaining tasks. Clarence Dunn is one rich man, and he has a lot of influence with the high and mighty crowd. Had Ramses screwed that up, our company's reputation would've never recovered. That fact ignited my fury at him all over again.

"What the hell is this?"

All I'd done since I walked into the office this morning was yell about Ramses and his inability to control himself. But that note? That note took the fucking cake.

"What's wrong?" Thomas asked, suddenly standing in my doorway.

"Ramses has to attend *a ball* with them?" I held the letter up and met Thomas's confused gaze. "He's honestly expected to be there?"

"Yes. He and I spoke briefly about this. With all the time he's spent at their house and at their events, they'd consider it as a slight against them if he didn't show. If he's not back in time, you'll have to go in his place to represent the partnership."

"Perfect," I spat out sardonically. "Just fucking

perfect."

"It's only a couple of weeks away. My advice is to have your formal clothes prepared as soon as possible."

"Agreed. I don't expect him to return anytime soon."

Slade Barnett, August 1790

As expected, Ramses is still nowhere to be found. Neither hide nor hair of him anywhere. As usual, I've had to pick up the slack he left behind and carry both my weight and his with the business. Thomas's assistance has been invaluable, and I'm sorely tempted to kick Ramses's ass out and give Thomas his half of the partnership. My only hesitation in doing it is Ramses is still my brother, regardless of how pissed off I am.

"Tonight is the ball. I presume you're prepared to attend?" Thomas asked as he walked into my office.

"I'm as ready as I'll ever be. You know how I detest dances and masquerade balls and formal affairs. The pretentious elite never fail to show up in droves, anxious for everyone beneath them to kiss their asses."

"Ah, but the lovely Miss Alea Dunn will be there tonight. She is a beautiful sight to behold. She'll be eighteen next month, and she's exactly your type.

The talk around town is she plans to quietly dissolve her engagement to her betrothed in England. Now, all the young bucks in their upper-class circles are vying for her hand and will most likely chase her around the ballroom all night."

"Bucks in rut season, huh?" I chuckled.

"Exactly. But they're no match for you."

"Why are you trying to marry me off to some young girl I've never even met? As a matter of fact, why are you trying to marry me off at all?"

Thomas shrugged one shoulder, and one side of his mouth lifted in amusement. "You've been a bachelor long enough. And you work too much. You need to take some time for fun."

"Having a wife is not my idea of fun, Thomas. I have plenty of fun after work without having the burden that comes with a wife."

Thomas walked off, but I didn't miss how he laughed under his breath. Like he knew something I didn't.

Turns out, Thomas did know something I didn't. First, I don't give his visions of the future nearly enough credit. But the bastard didn't tell me what he'd seen, or how going to the ball tonight would change my life forever. I owe him an ass-kicking for that—then a brotherly embrace immediately afterward.

So many times before I left my house tonight, I considered sending a note expressing my regret to Clarence because some fake emergency needed my immediate attention. But I didn't because Thomas's words reverberated in my mind. The Dunns would view it as a personal slight after all the business they've given Ramses, and by extension, me. Reconciled to accept a night of sheer torture, I donned my best formal clothing and took my carriage to the grand ballroom at the Imperial Renaissance Hotel.

The events of the evening are clearer to me now than when I first experienced them, so I'm capturing my memories while they are still fresh. I say that as if I could ever truly forget, when in truth, I keep a detailed account of my thoughts and interactions for more than just my own sake. Should anything happen to me, I'd like to think my experiences will help others of my kind not to make the same mistakes I've made. Learn from the things I've learned. Even though I've been an immortal for decades now, I learned what forever truly means tonight.

The very second I walked into the ballroom, a force unlike anything I'd ever experienced hit me with the full strength of a hurricane. Feelings I'd never experienced swirled all around me, simultaneously confounding me and providing vivid clarity. A heavy weight settled in my chest around my dead heart. Had I not known better, I would've sworn it started beating again, thumping against my ribcage like a strong man swinging a sledgehammer. My lungs burned for oxygen, forcing me to inhale deeply, though I don't need it to survive.

I didn't ask anyone where to find the Dunns' table. My feet carried me straight to the source of my sudden and intense obsession. The instant our eyes met, the connection between us was sealed. Our separate destinies were fused into a singular conclusion. Fate had brought us together against all odds in the vastness of time and chance. Though we hadn't met, names hadn't been exchanged, and our numerous questions hadn't been asked, the impossible became possible.

The other half of me, my immortal love, sat directly in front of me. The depths of her soft brown eyes sparkled with interest. Her long blond hair lay across her bare shoulders in loose curls. The shimmer of her black silk formal gown paled in comparison to her radiance. I tried to speak, to introduce myself, to save myself from the awkward situation I'd created, but my voice was mute.

"Are you Slade Barnett, Ramses's brother?"

The voice came from a man at the table, but it took considerable effort to untether my eyes from hers. She had them physically restrained by just *being*.

"Yes, I am. Ramses sends his apologies for missing such a delightful event, but pressing matters require his presence elsewhere. You have my full attention and commitment," I replied.

The man stood and extended his hand. "Clarence Dunn. It's very nice to finally meet you in person. You've worked with several close friends of mine, and they've done nothing but sing your high praises. I have no doubts whatsoever of your abilities to effectively manage my shipping contracts. But we'll save that for next week. We're here strictly to enjoy each other's company. We've saved you a seat at our table. Dinner will be served soon."

Had another man been seated beside the young lady who had me under her spell, I would've insisted he move at that point. But further confirming fate indeed had her hand on us, the empty chair was beside my as-yet-unnamed love. She watched me intently and held her breath as I approached, only releasing it when I took my place at her side.

"Slade, this is my wife, Frances," he gestured to the lovely lady to his right. "And seated beside you is our daughter, Alea."

He continued around the table, introducing me to other men and women in his elite circle. Though I heard every word and memorized every name, my focus never strayed from the striking beauty beside me. The chatter around the table started back up. Several of the ladies were involved in one conversation, while the men carried on a different one.

Alea and I remained in our own distinct world.

"I hope you don't think this is too forward of me, but you are absolutely stunning. I've never seen a more beautiful lady in my life."

"Thank you. That's very kind of you to say." Her cheeks became a rosy red, her pulse spiked, but she kept her eyes locked on mine despite her shy nature.

The music paused as the band prepared to change to a hauntingly beautiful slow song. On impulse, I stood and extended my hand to her. "Would you do me the honor of sharing this dance with me?"

When she put her soft hand in mine, time stood still.

"Alea?" Her mother's questioning eyes alternated between Alea, me, and our entwined hands.

"Slade and I are going to dance to this song. We'll return to the table well in time to enjoy the meal," Alea replied as she stood.

Clarence leaned back in his chair, studied us for a moment, and the corner of his mouth lifted slightly. The pride that showed through his eyes was solely intended for Alea. Frances jerked her head to look at him, undoubtedly for him to object, but he gave us his nod of approval instead.

"Frances, my love, you know I've always had an uncanny ability to quickly determine a man's intentions. I have an exceptionally good feeling about Slade."

I smiled and nodded my appreciation to him. "Thank you, sir. That means a great deal to me."

Before anything else could be said, I led Alea to the dance floor. With one hand on her waist and the other holding her hand close to our faces, I began to sway with her in time with the melodic music. She felt so good, so right, in my arms, it was almost overwhelming. Add to that the sweet scent of her skin plus the warmth of her touch, and it's a miracle I didn't whisk her away from the party in that moment.

"At the risk of sounding like a lunatic," I started. "You feel it too. Don't you?"

Her eyes flew open wide for a split second before understanding dawned and her expression softened. "I felt it before I ever saw your face. It was as if my soul suddenly felt a part of itself enter the room and began desperately calling out. When you first stepped into the doorway, I knew you were the one my soul needed to feel whole again. I knew you were the one my soul recognized as part of itself."

"Exactly," I whispered, astonished she so perfectly captured my feelings. "You are my immortal love, Alea. You don't understand the full meaning of that right now. You probably also question how I can claim love when we barely know each other's name. But you can believe me when I say this. You will understand it all. Very soon."

"I believe you."

With everything I needed to say and wanted to ask, none of it seemed as important as just holding her and enjoying every second of it. We moved with flawless and effortless precision around the floor without conversation for the rest of the song. We shared all of our thoughts and feelings through longing gazes and gentle touches. It was more than enough, especially since we were both trying to wrap our heads around what was happening.

When the song ended, we rejoined the group at the table, and I was pleased to see smiles on her parents' faces as we took our seats.

"That was amazing!" Frances exclaimed before anyone could speak.

"What was?" Alea asked, her confusion etched in her features.

"The way you two danced—it was as if you'd practiced all your life. Yet, your technique was unlike anyone else," Frances explained.

Alea and I exchanged glances, and she shrugged her shoulders. "I'm not sure what you mean, Mother. It was just a simple dance."

The hotel staff saved us from Frances pressing the topic when they placed the first course of the meal in front of us. Polite conversation resumed, and our display was soon forgotten. When I finally found my voice, all the questions I couldn't bring myself to ask while dancing created an easy dialogue with

Alea. Several times throughout dinner, I noticed Clarence watching us with an openly amused look on his face. I would say I'm thankful it wasn't a look of disdain, but it wouldn't have stopped me either way. He never interjected his opinion, never interrupted our chatting, but he still watched, as any good father would do. By the end of the dessert course, Alea and I had learned almost everything there was to know about the other.

Almost. There are a couple of important facts I still need to share with her when the time is right.

The end of the evening came much too soon. I wasn't anywhere near ready to leave her, and she wasn't ready to leave me. We stood outside the hotel entrance and waited for her parents to finish saying their goodbyes.

"Usually, these things feel like they take days to come to an end," she said with a twinge of sadness. "This is the first one I can remember wishing would last longer. The time has passed by so quickly. It feels like we just arrived, and we're already leaving."

"So true." I nodded. "I began the evening looking for an excuse not to come at all. Now I'm desperate to find any excuse never to leave."

"Come by the house tomorrow, Slade. We'll finalize the contract you sent via courier, and we'll talk about next steps," Clarence said as he escorted his wife out. "I trust your coachman is retrieving your carriage?"

"Yes, sir. He's actually waiting for me on the opposite side of the drive." I nodded my head toward where my carriage awaited, but I couldn't bring myself to leave Alea to climb into it.

"Would you mind seeing Alea home first? My wife and I would sincerely appreciate your assistance."

"It would be my pleasure, sir. She's safe with me."

He inhaled deeply and gave me a pointed look. "I wouldn't trust you with my only daughter if I didn't already know that, Slade."

Clarence and Frances climbed into their carriage, and I signaled for my coachman to pull my carriage around. The smile Alea sported lit her entire face and made me smile in return. Once we were alone in the carriage behind the closed door, she turned toward me to speak, but my mouth had other activities in mind. An impulsive craving for her consumed me, and I couldn't control it.

Our lips clashed in a frantic kiss. Need and desire drove us to reckless actions for a girl of her stature and family name. But if I'm honest, that was the last thing on my mind at the time. Her lips were so soft, and they were made solely for me. My hands cupped her face and tilted her head to the side to deepen the kiss. My tongue swiped across the part in her lips, causing her to gasp lightly, and giving me the access I needed to completely own her mouth.

My tongue slid across hers, like silk on silk, gliding with grace and natural beauty in a heated, sensual dance. Her initial shock was quickly replaced with yearning, and she gripped my shirt tightly in her delicate fingers, pulling me closer and closer to her. I slid my mouth and tongue along her jawline, leaving a swath of hot kisses in my wake, and moved down to her neck. The scent of her blood mixed with the scent of her skin was a highly addictive aphrodisiac. When I slid down the sensitive skin of her neck, licking, sucking, nipping, she moved her hands to my head and gripped my hair, releasing a needful whimper.

The carriage stilled, and I knew we'd reached the end of our journey for the evening.

"Until tomorrow, then?" I asked, my lips touching hers.

"You'll be in my dreams tonight," she promised.

I walked her to the front door of her house and made sure she was safely inside before returning to my coach.

Now that I've given her family enough time to fall asleep, I'm returning to her house.

Indeed, you will dream of me tonight, my love. Within seconds, I'll be in your bedroom with you. I'll make sure you have the most fantastic dreams.

Chapter Six

Alea, September 1790

The last several weeks have been a whirlwind of activities, one event leading to the next, and all spiraling out of control in the most delicious and welcome ways. At the epicenter of the storm that has taken me by surprise and surpassed any expectation I could possibly dream up is the man who holds my heart in his very hands—Slade Barnett.

When Slade first approached the table the night of the ball, I was completely tongue-tied and completely under his spell. He has the same thick brown hair as his brother, but a light smattering of a beard outlines his handsome face. His eyes are dark, mystifying, and penetrating. It was the way he carried himself that set him apart from every other handsome man in the room. He wore confidence and tenacity the way other men wore overcoats, and the others in the room seemed to sense it as he walked by them.

Over the last five weeks, we've spent every day together. At first, our interactions were strictly on a friendly level, just getting to know each other and enjoying the time we spent together. Even so, I knew there was more to my feelings for him than I'd admit to anyone else. When he brought me home after the ball, he kissed me in a way I'd never been kissed before. The touch of his lips on mine set my skin on fire. I'd never felt such longing before. It traveled through my body straight to the area between my legs. The lightning bolt of desire that hit me came out of nowhere and was the most intense feeling I'd ever experienced.

Until I fell asleep that night.

I dreamt of him all night. My dreams were so clear and vivid I would've put my hand on the Bible and sworn they were real. In my dream, I was asleep in my bed, and everything in my bedroom was in its exact correct place. A slight noise woke me, and he was standing at the foot of my bed when I opened my eyes.

"Slade?" I asked, my voice groggy from sleep.

"Yes, it's just me, Alea. No need to be alarmed, my love."

"If my dad hears you...if he finds you in here, he'll kill you." Immediately wide awake, I couldn't hide the alarm in my voice or the fear in my eyes.

"He won't hear us. He won't know I'm here. Tell me now if you want me to go, and I will."

His voice was smooth, reassuring, and even in my dream, I felt my mind falling under his trance. His beautiful eyes bored through me, seeing straight into my thoughts before he took control of them with gentle, persuasive nudges. If I'm honest with myself, he didn't actually control me, he simply released any inhibitions I had.

"I don't want you to go, Slade. I want you to stay."

His smile covered his gorgeous face, but the predatory nature of it made my skin pebble in waves, matching the chills that ran up and down my spine. "I'm so glad to hear you say that, Alea. Let me show you how much."

He put his hands on my bed and crawled up my body until he barely hovered over me. When I spoke, our lips brushed together, and it was all I could do to stop myself from being the instigator. "How did you get in here?"

"You invited me in. Remember?"

His lips covered mine, and his tongue dipped into my mouth. His taste was exquisite and addictive. The more I had, the more I wanted, the greedier I became, and the more aggressive I grew.

When I felt his smile against my lips, there was no doubt he knew how much he affected me.

Before I knew it, my bedcovers were pulled back and I was only covered by my nightgown. His hands slid down the fabric that molded against my body. When his fingers reached the hem, he lifted it over my head without ever leaving my body. I was fully exposed to him, and it didn't bother me in the least. I wasn't shy, I wasn't ashamed, I wasn't embarrassed.

I was emboldened.

My hands roamed over his body, reveling in the dips and ridges of his muscular physique. The silky strands of his hair flowed freely between my fingers. It was the first time I'd touched a man in that manner, even if it was a dream, and I liked it. No, I loved it. The strength he projected, yet his touch was tender. The masculine way he took control, yet freely gave me the reins to make the decisions.

When his mouth covered my bare breast, my ability to think was stripped from my mind. The sensation of the warmth of his tongue wrapped around my nipple was amazing. He sucked it deep into his mouth; the mixture of pleasure and pain from him pulling it between his teeth elicited my moan of approval.

"Has anyone ever touched you like this, Alea?"

"No. Never," I answered breathily.

"Do you like it? Or do you want me to stop?"

"I don't want you to stop." And I didn't. The physical pleasure was too much to tell him to stop what he was doing.

His mouth moved to my other breast and lavished attention on it while his hand squeezed and massaged its twin. Then his hand began moving, slow and torturous movements across my chest and down my stomach, until it rested between my thighs. Deviously close to where I wanted him to finish what he'd started. Wickedly near touching me where I've never even touched myself, but where I want to experience it for the first time with him.

"I want to teach you everything you don't know. I want you to experience everything for the first time with me. Only with me, Alea. I'll make you feel things you've never even dreamed of before. All I ask is that you put your full trust in me. You won't be sorry."

Then his fingers began to move through the curls that covered me.

"You're so focused on being a proper little lady. You don't have to pretend with me, my love. You want my fingers in your pussy, but you don't want to say it. Your body craves my touch so much I'd say you're already wet just from thinking about it. Tell me what you want me to do, Alea."

Did I want him to do that? Did I want him to touch me there?

"My willpower is infinite, sweetheart. I can hold

my hand right here for hours without giving you what you want. But if you make me wait that long, you'll wish you hadn't."

His threat was both chilling and sexy, scaring me and arousing me at the same time. "I want you to touch me."

"That's not what I want to hear."

I knew what he wanted me to say. Without ever verbalizing it, I knew what he expected to hear from me. Gentle nudges in my mind spurred me on, encouraged me, and reassured me. "I want you...to put your fingers in my pussy."

"I've got a better idea." He slid down my body with slow, calculated moves while his eyes remained riveted to mine.

"What are you doing, Slade?" I whispered.

"Keep your eyes on me, and watch what I do to you. Watch everything. Don't close your eyes."

I watched with rapt attention as he moved into position, his fingers parted the folds between my legs, and the heat from his tongue connected with what felt like every nerve ending in my body. Shudders tore through my body as he licked me and thrust his tongue inside me, rolling it around and groaning against my skin.

"You taste so good I can barely control myself. I love fucking you with my tongue." His words made my heart flutter, and my body released an unexpected surge of wetness. He moaned appreciatively and became more vigorous in his quest.

My fingers gripped his hair, and I held on tightly while I watched everything he did to me. When a scream tore free from my throat, a fleeting thought of waking my parents quickly vanished and was replaced with the most delectable gratification. When the ability to think and speak returned, I was at a loss for words to describe how incredible he'd made me feel.

"How? What? I don't understand—" My stammering made no sense. My thoughts were jumbled, and I didn't know where to even start to understand.

"You've no doubt seen pictures in books. Naughty books your family or friends have hidden in their libraries."

He waited for my answer, but I could only nod in agreement. I had seen a couple of them in recent years. My father has one hidden in his office I stumbled across when looking for something else. The drawn depictions of various acts both embarrassed and intrigued me. Then when we were visiting his brother's estate, one of my older cousins showed me a similar book, and we giggled over the different positions the characters were drawn in.

"Did you like this?" he asked, but he knew the answer. The smirk he wore told me there was no sense in trying to argue the point.

"Yes," I whispered with eagerness.

"We can do this again...and more. Every night, Alea. I can lift you up to the heavens and bring you safely back to earth again. Just give me the word."

"Every night?" My eyes grew wide with the thought and anticipation of such a divine promise.

"Every night. This is only the beginning."

"I'll wait for you here, then. Meet me here, every night."

He rose up on all fours and crawled back over my naked body. He dipped his head and drove his tongue deep into my mouth. Even in my dream, I could taste the mixture of Slade and myself on his tongue, and it only made me want more. "Until tomorrow night, then," he promised when he broke our kiss.

When I woke the next morning, my gown covered my body and my bedcovers were undisturbed. It was the most surreal feeling because the dream felt like it actually happened. When he came to visit later that day, my mother was concerned I had come down with something because my face was so flushed. It took quite a bit of reassuring her I felt fine and it was probably just something I'd eaten.

At least a couple of times, I thought I'd caught Slade stifling a laugh behind his cup of tea. When I challenged him on it, his shocked and confused reaction appeared genuine, so I dropped it. I think that was the only time I actually met his gaze head on that day. Visions of what we'd done in my dream replayed in my mind every other time I'd tried.

Regardless of my internal embarrassment, we've continued our daily courtship, and every day is better than the last. My father absolutely adores Slade and, in a completely shocking move, now allows Slade to take me out on official dates without a chaperone. I'm sheltered, protected, and loved when I'm with him, but in a completely different way than my family treats me. Slade doesn't put me on a shelf, protecting me like a delicate china doll the way my father does. He shelters and protects me when needed, but he also teaches me to be independent and confident in my own abilities.

We were walking through the park one day, and a couple of shady characters stepped into the path in front of us. They were lying in wait for us to approach, and my heart began to pound in my chest. My instincts were to turn away and walk as fast as possible back in the opposite direction. Slade stopped me and brushed his hand along my cheek.

"Do you trust me, my love?"

"Of course," I replied.

"Then walk with me. Don't be afraid of them."

"But Slade—"

He put his finger over my lips to stop my objection, looked deep into my eyes, and comforted me. "I'm with you. Nothing and no one can hurt you while I'm with you."

With my life in his hands, we continued our

stroll. Slade continued speaking as if he hadn't a care in the world. My eyes were glued to the two men on the path in front of us. They'd split up and were waiting on opposite sides, waiting to ambush us and to do God knows what else to us. The bigger of the two spoke first.

"You don't belong in this area of the park. This is our path. It'll cost you to pass." His eyes raked up and down my body, undressing me as they moved, and his lips curled into an ugly sneer.

"It'll cost you more if you don't move on this instant," Slade replied, his voice low and dangerous. "Believe me, gentlemen. You won't like the price I charge."

He stepped in front of me to block me from their leering gazes. "And if you ever see this woman again—and look at her in that manner—I'll rip your eyes out of your fucking head and make you eat them for lunch."

The horrified expressions on the men's faces before they turned and ran away were all the reassurance I needed. Slade turned and wrapped his arm around my shoulders. "Let's finish our walk, shall we?"

"How did you do that? How did you make them run away like that?"

"I just showed them I'm not one they should try to antagonize. Maybe I'll teach you all my tricks and skills one day."

"As much as I'd love that, I doubt my threats would be as effective as yours," I laughed.

"You'd be surprised what you can accomplish, if you handle it just right."

That's just one example of what he's done for me over the past several weeks. Every night, he returns to me in my dreams. In every dream, he keeps his original promise. My body has been racked with sensations I never even knew were possible. I'm so fully sated and thoroughly worn out after I fall asleep in my dreams, I don't dream the rest of the night. It's been absolutely heavenly.

During our daytime excursions, it's become exceedingly hard to keep my night visions at bay. What would he think of me if I told him all the inappropriate dreams I've had about him, about us? Is something wrong with me, or are these kinds of dreams normal for young women of my age? I wouldn't know—and I have no one to ask, no one to talk to about it who won't immediately judge me.

It's times like this when I miss Sean so very much.

Even during his moody phase before he finally confided in me, he was still my friend. My only friend I could have an honest conversation with and not worry about how I'd be viewed later. Just thinking of Sean makes me miss him and wonder how he's doing. It's been so long since I've seen him. To think, we would be married by now had I stayed in London instead of coming to America.

And had I stayed, I wouldn't have met the wonderful man who has become my obsession—at my side by day, and in my dreams by night. If the last five weeks have taught me anything, it's that love doesn't abide by man's rule of time. My love for this man is strong, and it grows by leaps and bounds every single day.

Slade and Father had a long, private discussion before he left our house tonight. Though I tried to persuade one of them to tell me what was so important, neither of them would budge. Neither would give a hint of any kind. I couldn't even tell from their facial expressions if it was good or bad. It very well could've been something regarding their business dealings, as Ramses still hasn't returned to resume responsibilities for his part of the business.

I wonder if their talk concerned Ramses.

This guessing game is driving me mad.

Slade Barnett, 1790

What I'd always considered to be a fairy tale of epic proportions has proven to be one-hundred percent accurate. My immortal love is here—and she loves me in return.

After spending so much time with her and her family, certain human emotions were involved, and I found myself sincerely vying for her parents' approval. Tonight, all my schmoozing paid off. I don't have to kill them, after all. I'd already arranged for a private meeting with Clarence and expected more of a fight than I received. His love for Alea is strong, and that's one of the very things that makes him so focused and driven. Strong-willed people are much harder to influence.

"Come in, Slade. How are things going?" Clarence asked as I took a seat in his office.

He purposely left the question open for interpretation to avoid limiting the conversation. I both appreciated and respected him for that.

"Very well. Actually, that's what I wanted to speak with you about today. I think you know I'm thoroughly and completely in love with Alea. I believe when two people are destined to be together, nothing can keep them apart. Alea is my destiny. She is the one fate designed for me and only me. It's because of this I'd like your blessing to ask Alea to be my wife."

Clarence studied me with his serious scrutinizing expression for several seconds. Then his smile crawled across his face before he slapped his thighs with both hands.

"That's the best news I've heard in months! Even better than all the shipping deals you've given me. Better than all the new friends we've made in New York. You've made my daughter happier than anyone ever has. I'd be proud to call you my son,

Slade."

He circled around his desk and drew me into a fatherly embrace. After a couple of manly slaps on my back, he released me.

"When do you plan to ask her?"

"In a couple of days—on our outing this weekend. I have an exciting, romantic day planned for us," I assured him. He wanted to know his daughter would always be on a pedestal—and I have no problem with taking her up to unbelievable heights before gently bringing her back down to rest in my arms.

"Her mother and I will anxiously await the weekend and all the details of your exciting proposal."

We shook hands, and I left his office under the watchful eyes of Alea. My plans had to remain a secret until it was the right time, so I kept my facial expression impassive as I said my goodbyes. Her pensive expression from my refusal to share information cut me. It wasn't that she didn't trust me, but there are so many lingering questions and topics we haven't covered yet.

But we will.

For now, I need to feed.

Chapter Seven

Slade Barnett, 1790

Today went even better than I could have planned, imagined, or hoped for in my wildest dreams. And my dreams can get pretty wild. But apparently, Alea inspires my dreams more and more every day.

We started the morning early and took my carriage to a remote location a couple of hours outside the city. I picked a spot on the banks of the river to spend the day with the love of my life. My immortal love.

"Where are we going?" she asked, excitement ringing in her voice.

"I have a very important surprise for you today, sweetheart. We have the whole day together, and I don't plan on bringing you back until late tonight. You have no idea how long I've waited for this day."

She bounced in her seat playfully, her beautiful smile lit up her face, and her excitement was barely contained. But it was true—she had no idea how long I'd waited to find her. Never actually believing I would, but never able to fully give up hope that she existed.

"Are you not going to give me a hint where you're taking me?"

"No. But I do have you all to myself for the next two hours in this carriage. Then for the rest of the day when we reach our destination. Then again on the ride back. I will give you a hint of one of my many plans for you. I plan to take full advantage of our time alone."

Without reading her thoughts, I knew the visions from her nightly dreams flashed through her mind. Her pink-tinged cheeks and the way she averted her eyes were telltale signs, but I planned to help her past that embarrassment. Permanently.

As long as she didn't run away in the opposite direction, screaming in terror, after I confessed the truth to her. The whole truth about me and what I am. Inside, I knew that could never happen. The shock of it may take her a few minutes to absorb, but I knew she'd quickly adjust. The rest of the ride was spent with our mouths fused together, our hands wandering and pleasing, and my cock throbbing painfully behind the fabric of my pants. The need to make her completely mine surpassed painful weeks ago. Now it has become hell on earth.

But I won't take her—until she knows the truth. The nights I've visited her in her dreams and in her bed, I've shown more restraint than I ever knew was possible. I'm definitely the most powerful fucking vampire in the entire fucking world. There's no other explanation for how I was able to resist the strongest temptation known to man. Or vampire.

A knock on the carriage door alerted me we'd reached our destination. My coachman opened the door at my command, and I stepped out first. I extended my hand to help her out. "Ready to see where we are?"

"I can't wait. But for the record, as long as I'm with you, it'll be perfect wherever we are."

I leaned in and kissed her. "I love you, Alea."

She knew, but hearing the words made it all so very real. "I love you too, Slade."

She stepped out of the carriage with my help and immediately gasped. Her hand flew over her mouth, and her eyes grew wide. She took a couple of steps and turned slowly as she took in the scenery. My servants traveled ahead a day early and prepared everything for our arrival. The white canvas tent was erected on the banks of the river. Autumn flowers adorned the outside and lined the white rug that served as a walkway to the tent opening.

The clear water ran swiftly beside the covering and provided the perfect backdrop to the scenic vista surrounding us. She took carefully measured steps along the water, no doubt memorizing every sight and sound along the way. I walked behind her—memorizing everything about this momentous occasion. There wasn't one moment I wanted to forget.

Inside, the tent was arranged just as spectacularly as the outside. The plush, plump cushions matched the fall flower colors—deep yellows, oranges, and browns—and were arranged several deep along three full walls to make large, comfortable lounge areas. The flowers decorated every surface, trays of finger foods in every variety sat on columns of varying heights, and flutes of the finest champagne sat beside the tray of specialty strawberries I'd had imported for just this occasion.

Having a household staff of immortal servants has its perks.

I led her to one of the chairs and motioned for her to sit, and I took my seat beside her after giving her one of the glasses of champagne. "Take a sip of your champagne," I instructed and she obliged. I then raised a strawberry up to her mouth. "Now bite." I offered the red berry and watched spellbound as her teeth sank into its sweet flesh.

"That is so delicious," she gushed. "The sweetness from the champagne and strawberry mixed is amazing."

I captured her mouth and drove my tongue inside to taste the sweetness for myself—but with her distinct flavor mixed in. When I broke away, I swung down on one knee in front of her and began my prepared speech.

"Alea, my love. I want to ask you something, but there are things about me you must know first."

"No matter what you have to tell me about yourself, I'm sure I will love every word of it, Slade. As much as I love you."

Her response was so sweet, so filled with warmth and honesty, I was afraid my admission would break the spell of love we'd lived under.

"I hope that is true, Alea. But if not, you must promise to tell me. I need you to give me your word, on your honor."

"On my honor, I will tell you the truth. No matter what that means."

I scrubbed my hand over my face and took a deep breath while I worked up the nerve to tell her the whole truth about myself.

"Slade, just tell me. You know whatever you have to say won't change how I feel about you."

"Alea, I want to marry you. I want to spend the rest of my life with you. Day and night, I want you by my side. I've spoken with your father and explained the decision must be yours and yours alone, because there is a lot at stake—for both us.

"Many, many years ago, something happened to me that changed me forever. At first, I hated it. I despised what I had become and wished for nothing but death to take me. Eventually, though, I learned to accept my lot and embrace it.

"I'm glad I did now, because it brought me to you. Without this curse, I never would've been so lucky. When I explain this to you, there are a few things I need you to remember. First, this is not a joke. I'm not trying to be funny or charming in any way. Secondly, I know this will be hard to believe and accept, so if you want to take time to think it over, I'll gladly give you that. And lastly, no matter what your decision is or how you may look at me after I finish, you can never breathe a word of this to another person. Your life will be in dire risk if you do.

"Do you understand and agree to these terms?"

The serious turn her normally jovial expression took assured me she understood the gravity of my words. "I agree, Slade. Tell me what it is."

"I am a vampire, Alea. A creature of the night. One of the undead, the damned. We do exist, and there are many more like me. If you agree to marry me, you will have to join us. There's no other way to ensure your safety in the clan."

At first, she thought I was pulling a practical joke on her. Her sly smile and dubious expression conveyed her thoughts with precision. The only way to convince her what I said was true was to show her my true self. Her doubt was instantly replaced with fear before changing to a quiet comprehension as her fingers skimmed my changed features. I changed back as she watched, then continued explaining.

"Changing means you'll never grow any older than you are at the time of your vampire birth. You'll never grow old and feeble. You'll never be sick or develop any kind of disease, not even a common cold. You'll gain strength like you've never known before and eyesight to see clearly even in the blackest part of the night. You'll move as fast as you want with no effort at all. No human will ever be a threat to you, physically speaking."

"What else does it mean?" she whispered.

"My sweet Alea. Always so smart and inquisitive," I praised. "There are things you won't like, yes. Because we're not alive but not quite dead, we can never have children. You'll never feel the miracle of a baby growing in your body. You'll never experience the pain and magic of childbirth. You'll never know the bond of nursing a babe on your breasts.

"You'll have to feed on human blood. Whether you take a life or not is up to you—there are ways around it if you're careful. But it takes incredible willpower and strength to stop feeding once you're past a certain point. It's different for all of us, but it's there nonetheless.

"You can never tell your family what you've become. If you maintain contact with them, they'll ask why you haven't conceived a child. They'll notice you haven't aged, especially when their own mirror reflects the ravages of age. And as time marches on, you'll witness every human you know and love die while you live on.

"Your friends will be other vampires, for the most part. Our clan will become your family. Mortals won't understand us, and the questions become impossible to dodge. This way of life changes everything you know and all you've ever wanted in your current life. You have to know and understand that before you decide.

"In truth, I could force this on you and not give you the option. In doing so, it would absolve you of the burden I've put on you. But I love you too much for that. If your answer is no, there will never be another for me. No other woman will ever know my love and devotion. But you can still have everything you've ever dreamed of—a man who loves you, children, growing old together, and enjoying your grandchildren. You still have that option, because I love you enough to want you to be happy, regardless if that's with me or not."

Alea Dunn, October 1790

The wheels in my mind turned at a blinding speed as I absorbed his every word. When he first announced he was a vampire, my natural inclination said he was pulling a prank on me. It was my self-preservation kicking in, telling me not to play the fool and blindly believe him.

But that thought immediately vanished because he continued speaking, explaining the differences I could expect to experience after my vampire birth. That's when it hit me—he only listed the positive aspects of it, the things I could look forward to in my new reality. For every positive, there's a negative. For every give, there's a take. With all the new life had to give me, I had to know what it would take away.

My dreams of having a large family with several children filling my heart and my home?

Gone.

Looking forward to growing old with the love of my life, as is the natural progression?

Taken.

Watching my children grow into adults and have children of their own?

Vanished.

Large gatherings of family and friends during holidays and special events in their lives?

That could never be.

I sat motionless as the images of what might

have been played out in my mind's eye. I saw each one so clearly I could almost reach out and touch it. I felt the birth and loss of each child as surely as if I'd actually experienced it.

When I finally raised my eyes and met Slade's, everything faded away, becoming no more important than the background noise of the area that surrounded us. In his eyes, I saw my new future, and it was filled with new and exciting things I'd never known existed.

It held the promise of a love that would last a literal eternity. Love that could never diminish or fade. It would only grow stronger, and the bond would only become deeper. My soul knew what my mind couldn't comprehend at first.

None of my previous plans would work without Slade, because I could never be happy with anyone else. My life and death were bound to him in a way that could never be undone. He would let me go, giving me the opportunity to experience those things with someone else. But it would never be enough—because it would never be with him.

"I've known the truth since the moment I met you, Slade. You are my forever. Whether forever means in human form or as a vampire makes no difference to me. Without you, I wouldn't want to live another day.

"I can't pretend the thought of this doesn't scare my wits completely out of me. There's so much unknown. So much that doesn't fit into what I've believed to be true my whole life. All I know for certain is I can't see my future without you in it.

"But I must confess, I have so many questions. So many things I don't understand."

"Ask. Ask me anything. I'll tell you whatever you want to know."

"Vampires can't walk in the daylight. They don't eat food or drink wine. They kill everyone they see. They sleep in coffins, and they're cold, like a dead person. How is it none of these things applies to you?"

"I'm not cold because I drink blood from the living. Just like your blood gives you your warmth, blood saturates my tissues and keeps me warm. We don't kill everyone we see—we actually have very specific tastes in blood, much like your taste in food. There is a slight difference, though. You know how you can't resist some scents?"

"Yes," she whispered.

"We can't either. If we don't like a scent, it makes us angry, and that's who we feed on. If we like the scent, it gives more of a calming effect on us. Let's see, what other questions did you have? Oh yes, the daylight. That's not true—we can walk just fine in the light. Strong sunlight can make us slightly weaker, but it doesn't burn us. We don't sleep in coffins. We can eat and drink human food, but it won't sustain us like blood does. We'll die without blood, but we can live without food and water."

"So that's how I'd be too? I'd have to kill people and drink their blood to survive?"

"Yes. My answer is cold and direct because you have to come into this life with full knowledge of what you'll have to do, what you'll have to become. And it has to be your choice."

"My answer hasn't changed. My place is at your side. For all eternity. When does this happen? And how?"

"I'll change you myself, but not for several more years. You've just turned eighteen. If I turn you now, you'll always be this age. There's so much more you can experience as a human first, but still by my side. There are more changes your body will undergo as you mature. When the time is right, I'll explain everything about the process to you. For now, we'll plan our wedding like normal humans and let your parents enjoy every minute of it."

"My parents," I sighed. "How will I ever explain this to them?"

"You won't have to for a while, my love. When the time comes that our situation becomes evident, we'll discuss the best way to handle it. There are ways around it. So we can enjoy our time with them for now. I talked to your father before bringing you here. He knows I planned to propose today, and we have his blessing."

I leapt into his arms and kissed him all over his

face. To hear he'd taken the chance of talking to my father first, of asking for his approval and risking that my father would say no, made me feel cherished and loved. His main concern, his only concern, was my happiness. "When will we be married? I don't want to wait another day."

"I'm immortal, and there's no one I fear," he replied with confidence. "Except your mother where your wedding is concerned. That date, my love, will be up to you two."

The rest of the day and evening were more than I could've asked for. Slade was loving, thoughtful, and romantic in every gesture. Our walks by the river, the stroll through the woods, the time we spent alone in the extravagant tent. The way he refused to make love to me, even though I begged him without a shred of modesty or self-respect.

He admitted to the nights he snuck into my room. Some were times he entered my dreams. Some were times I was actually under his trance and I only thought it was a dream. When he confessed, I found I couldn't even be mad at him for the intrusion. Every dream and every encounter had just been too delicious and incredible to have an instant of regret.

When we returned and he said good night to my parents, I jumped into my father's arms and thanked him for his approval. He grinned and said he'd sent a letter to Sean's family when he first saw

Slade and me together. He knew Slade was the man for me at first sight and knew he should break the ties of my betrothal immediately. Then I kept my mom up half the night making wedding plans. I want to marry Slade as soon as possible—as quickly as we can pull everything together. Tomorrow sounded great to me, but for some reason, Mother refused to accept my request.

She did agree to one week, however, since the bulk of our family and friends are in the London area. The ceremony will be intimate and elegant, small and personal, quick and timeless. For the past week, my days have had new purpose and my nights have had new meaning. Every detail of my nuptials has been planned, every invitation has been hand-delivered, and every second hand of the clock seems to take longer to tick by.

Our wedding is tomorrow!

Ramses Barnett, 1790

Months. I've been gone for months. First, I tried feeding on animals in the forest, living like a wild animal myself. When that didn't satiate me, I resorted stalking people in the streets of the surrounding cities like a raving lunatic. All to try to get her scent out of my head. All to keep from ruining any chance of happiness and success for my brother and me. All to keep from drinking every last drop of that girl's blood, to keep from sinking my teeth into her perfectly smooth skin and getting off on the feel of it, and to hold on to the last shred of "human decency" I had in me. After all, she was still too young to turn—even too young to feed on unless there was no other option.

And I'd finally achieved my goal. I'd finally gotten her out of my system.

Until I returned to our city.

The scent of her blood hung over the streets like a heavy fog rolling in from the ocean. It wrapped around me like a thick cocoon and pushed my impulsiveness over the top. I had to have her. I couldn't fight it any longer. I couldn't wait another second. I couldn't survive one more night without the taste of her sweet blood in my mouth.

Like a moth to a flame, the pull to her family home drew me in, and I couldn't stop it. Even if I'd wanted to, which I didn't. I moved silently through the house like a stealthy animal stalking my prey. I loved the hunt—creeping up on my victim, pouncing when they least suspected it, watching the shock drain from their eyes as life left them. I loved it even more when they fought me tooth and nail, trying to hold on to life with every shred of strength they possessed. It makes it even sweeter when I win.

And I always win.

When I reached her room, she wasn't there. She hadn't slept there in weeks—her scent was barely distinguishable. She didn't live there anymore.

My feet seemed to move faster than light or sound in my quest to find her. On my obsessed hunt, I spent most of the night tracking her scent from place to place until it finally led me to the house where the scent was the strongest. It was her unique scent, mixed with the aromatic scent of feminine arousal.

When I finally stopped, it took several heartbeats—her heartbeats, to be exact—to realize exactly where I stood.

I watched as another man enjoyed the pleasures she provided in his bed. She straddled his hips, rolling hers back and forth as she rode him with her head thrown back in ecstasy. He reveled in the sensations her perfect body provided. He relished every whimper and wisp of her scent.

He was my brother.

She was my obsession.

My brother Slade was fucking Alea, my immortal obsession.

Chapter Eight

Ramses Barnett, 1790

In the haze of lunacy surrounding me during my search for Alea, I didn't even notice where I was until I saw Slade's face. There was no recognition of his house. There was nothing familiar about his street. My only focus was to find Alea—following her scent wherever it led me. When I was able to think clearly again, the sight of my brother with the object of my affection pushed me over the edge of sanity and into a place I've never been.

And where I hope never to be again.

The rage built inside me to unbelievable levels. All I could think about was killing my brother for betraying me and how good the last drop of his little whore's blood would taste as it slid down my throat.

They could spend eternity in hell together for all I cared. The only reason I didn't barge in and exact my revenge on the spot was because the heavy fog surrounding my brain cleared enough for me to remember my brother's strength far exceeded mine. As do his focus and determination. Had I ambushed him and his little wife, he would've killed me before I could inflict any damage on him.

No. My revenge took some planning to effectively carry out. When I make my move, every aspect must be so carefully calculated that every possible scenario has been considered. It had to be so thorough that nothing would be left of them to piece back together.

That time had come at last. It took weeks of waiting and watching. But finally, I made my move. Slade still hadn't turned Alea. I had no idea why he'd waited, but I smelled her blood long before I reached their house. It was almost as if fate herself had smiled down on me. The one thing I wanted so badly I could barely function—especially all the weeks when I was in her presence—was now within my grasp.

Slade was out of town on one of his business trips. Alea had planned to go with him, but her mother became ill with influenza. Such a serious condition these days without the proper care. Alea couldn't leave her in good conscience. Slade, being the man he's always been, insisted she stay home, and he'd cut his trip short to rush back as soon as he could.

That still left plenty of time for me to carry out my plan.

On my command, my personal army of vampires moved in on the Dunns' residence. Alea had been staying there at her mother's bedside since the morning Slade left. This is where she'd become mine—where it all started, where I put all the time in to win her trust, to capture her heart, and eventually take all I wanted from her.

We moved through the walls and windows as wisps of smoke. Our normal movements are too fast for the human eye to register, making it all too easy to move among the staff without being detected. I followed her scent to her parents' bedroom. Behind that closed door was the one woman who hadn't left my thoughts from the first day I locked on to her scent. With my anticipation at an all-time high, I moved through the door and prepared to drink my fill.

Clarence and Frances were in the bed asleep. But Alea was nowhere to be found. Her scent was still so strong in the room I would've sworn she was still there. The only explanation was I'd missed her by mere seconds. The clip-clop of horse's feet echoed from the driveway below the master bedroom windows. Clarence turned over, wrapped his arm around his wife's waist, and pulled her close to him.

"I'm glad you feel better now, my dear," he told Frances. "Alea hasn't slept in the room with us since she was a toddler. I haven't slept well in the last several nights, knowing she was likely awake and watching you. It was unnerving."

They both laughed, the love and appreciation for their only child still evident in their tones, before Frances replied. "She helped me get over it much faster than I would've without her. Still, I'm glad she was able to go home tonight. She wanted to be there when her husband gets home."

That was all I needed to hear.

The telepathic connection I have with my army of changelings is strong. I can send out a command through a single thought, and they will obey. When Frances referred to Slade with such a loving, approving tone after they'd shunned me as a suitor for their daughter, I issued the command.

My family, my clan, swooped in on the Dunn household staff and ripped their throats out. Not one of them stopped until the very last drop of blood remained in their veins. Until every servant had one foot in the grave and the other on sinking sand. Then they turned them—each and every one of them—and added them to our clan. The entire household, except for Clarence and Frances. They were mine, and I'm not one for sharing what's mine.

Frances was frozen in terror as she watched me feed on her husband. Her eyes were wide open, along with her mouth. She wanted to scream, but physically couldn't. She tried to make sense of what was happening, but mentally couldn't. She tried to reason with her rational mind that she was in a horrible nightmare, but realistically couldn't.

Though my vampiric features change my appearance to a degree, I'm still easily identified by those who know me. Frances and Clarence knew me well—but they still couldn't fully appreciate the irony of the situation. Because they couldn't fully believe it was actually me. They lost all capacity for logical analysis of the situation when they watched me change before their eyes.

Clarence fell limp on the bed, his body completely drained of blood. His eyes were open and fixed in death. Frances stared at him, slack-jawed and trembling uncontrollably. Her eyes strayed up to my face, and she started shaking her head from side to side. Denial took over as she shut down mentally. She could only whisper "no" repeatedly.

It made me smile.

"Yes, Frances. This is happening. It's not a terrible nightmare you'll tell Clarence all about tomorrow morning. It's not your imagination playing tricks on you. You're not going insane. In fact, you're not going anywhere. Ever again. If it's any consolation, neither is your daughter. You'll all meet again in the afterlife. Nothing to worry your pretty little head over."

Before she could respond, I sank my fangs into her neck and pulled her blood through the hollow points of my teeth. Her fingers curled into my shirt and gripped tightly—the epitome of the term "death grip"—until I'd drained so much of her life that she was unable to maintain her hold on me any longer. Her hands fell to her sides, and her body became lax in my arms. I listened with enraptured attention as her thundering heartbeat slowed to barely a crawl before it stopped completely. I released my hold on her, and she slumped to the bed, landing partly on top of Clarence.

Fitting—they lived together, died together, and rested in peace together.

My clan and I left the Dunns' and sprinted to Slade's house. His staff was immortal, so we'd have more of a fight when we converged on them. But after our thorough feeding, I felt ready to take on anyone and anything.

While my clan surprised Slade's servants with their strategic attacks, I went straight for my immortal obsession. Alea slept in their bedroom, unaware of the war that raged in the rest of her home. I moved through the door and froze in my tracks. She was scantily dressed in the sexiest see-through nightgown I'd ever seen. Her perky round breasts were on full display, her nipples already hard from the cool night breeze that wafted through the partially opened window. Her long hair was fanned out on the pillow under her head, and her beautiful neck was fully bared, just for my taking.

My mind warred with my thirst. Her body was as perfect and as tempting as her blood. The intense lust I felt toward her in no way stopped with the fluid flowing through her veins. I thought I might die if I didn't fuck her before I killed her. At least once, I needed to feel my cock buried deep in her perfect, tight pussy before I watched the light fade from her eyes.

Did I say just once? One time would have only made me want more. Since time was of the essence and Slade could show up at any time, I knew I had to control myself and my libido, or I'd get us both killed.

It would take my entire clan and me to restrain Slade once he realized what had happened; I knew that deep down in my psyche. Regret filled me over the loss of the pleasure of Alea's body. I'd never know it. I'd never experience it firsthand. My only consolation was the different kind of pleasure I'd have with her. In the blink of an eye, I covered her body with mine. In her sleep-filled state, she understandably confused me for her husband.

"Slade, I'm so glad you're home early," she purred, her eyes still closed. "I waited up for you as long as I could. But I'm glad you woke me."

"Tell me something, Alea. Do you let Slade drink your blood when he's fucking your pussy?

Has he tasted all of you? I do wish I had time to do it myself. But since you expect him home any second now, I suppose I've missed my chance."

Her eyes flew open in shock and horror then quickly changed to anger and determination. Though she knew what I was and what I could do—what I would do—she wasn't going down without a fight. She'd do her best to inflict her own kind of damage, even though I knew she couldn't hurt me.

"Your feistiness turns me on even more, Alea. I do wish I could show you just how much. It's really a shame how your friend Sean can't be with us."

Her face blanched as her eyes darted between mine.

"How do you know that name?"

"I know more than his name. It's sad, really. Somehow, his little secret got out, and they hanged him just a few days ago. Do you think they would hang me for 'unnatural acts' if they knew all the things I wanted to do to you?"

With an angry scream, she swung her fist toward my face as she lifted her upper body off the bed. I grabbed her arm and easily stopped her struggle. While she was suspended in midair, I took the perfect opportunity to finish what I'd started.

My fangs slid out.

My fingers skimmed across her scalp and gripped the base of her hair.

With a gentle tug, I pulled her head to the side

and exposed her long, smooth neck.

Then I leaned down, taking an extra second or two to rub my nose along her skin and inhale her intoxicating scent.

With painstaking control and precision, I sank my fangs into her neck, puncturing her skin with my needle-sharp teeth, and drew her heady and invigorating blood into my mouth.

That was heaven. Pure bliss. Nirvana.

That was where all the lore and tales originated from—the pure ecstasy of her taste, her scent, and her energy was what heaven must be made of. There's no other explanation. With Alea, I didn't want it to end. I never wanted to stop. I wanted to keep her for all time and drink from her whenever I desired, which would be daily at a minimum. I wanted all of her blood all to myself for the rest of her life.

That idea had merit. I could make it work. I could keep her, along with others, and establish a new system. A new way of feeding and living as a vampire could be so easy to establish. These thoughts flew through my mind at lightning speed as her blood slid down my throat.

Then my question from just a minute before reverberated through my mind and rang in my ears. The fury it evoked rose up inside me and fueled my original plan even more.

Do you let Slade drink your blood when he's

fucking your pussy?

Had he tasted her blood yet?

Had he taken all of what was supposed to be mine?

Had she willingly given him all of what was mine—what should have always been mine?

At that moment, I decided she couldn't live. I couldn't let her. I couldn't keep her if he'd tasted her blood before me. So I increased my efforts and drained her blood faster. Much like with her mother, I listened as her heartbeat changed. The fast, scared thumping started first, then it slowed as the volume of fluid in her body decreased, until the end drew near and it became barely audible.

Without warning, I found myself flying through the air and slamming into the wall on the opposite side of the room. Caught off guard from the surprise attack, my eyes first darted back to where Alea lay still on the bed. Thomas, Slade's right-hand man, was covering her body with a blanket and lifting her off the bed. In my confusion, at first, I thought he was trying to take her for himself. A sharp jab to my face followed by a searing hot pain in my neck nearly brought me to my knees.

That pain could only come from the silver blade of a knife at my throat.

There's only one man on earth who could do that to me.

My brother.

Thomas and Alea were gone, and Slade was so angry, so vicious, he moved faster than even I could see. The cries from my clan streamed through my mind, and I immediately ordered their retreat. They didn't stand a chance against him in his blind rage.

Regret and shame filled me as I came out of my crazed state and realized the full ramifications of my actions. Though I hated to add more pain to my brother, distracting him was the only way I could keep him from killing me.

"Slade, I know you're in here and you want to kill me. I can't blame you for that. But your wife is close to death, and I think you should go to her before it's too late. You'll never forgive yourself if you're in here fighting with me rather than at her side when she breathes her last. I'm immortal. I have all the time in the world. I'll always be around later if you want to resume this."

His voice was low and controlled when he replied. He was deadlier than I'd ever seen or heard him in all the decades upon decades we'd been vampires. Rather than the normal blue vampiric hue, his eyes were a deep red. I've never seen that happen with any other vampire and I had no idea what to make of it. "Your time just ran out. Immortality won't last much longer for you."

Slade rushed out of the room to get to Alea's side before her heart completely stopped for good. I moved to the window outside and watched Alea,

Slade, and Thomas.

Slade drew her limp body into his arms, their chests pressed together, and he buried his tear-soaked face into her hair. His cries of pain and heartbreak echoed off the buildings all over the neighborhood. I had to leave at that point. I couldn't bear to watch what I'd done to my brother. When the devastation subsided and the real anger took its place, I would meet a side of my brother I'd never seen before.

He'll come after me with a new vengeance, a renewed purpose, and more strength than imaginable.

And he'll be coming for my head.

Chapter Nine

Slade Barnett, 1790

I am going to kill my brother.

He's not even my brother anymore.

He ceased being my brother in any way when he attacked my wife and my household. He betrayed me in a way no one else could have. The total disregard he had for me, the complete lack of brotherly love he displayed toward me, and the cold, calculated way he planned his assault showed me more proof than I'd ever need to see.

When I came home from my business trip, I knew in an instant something was terribly wrong.

I'd saved Ramses from his crazy alter ego before. He changed into what could only be described as a mindless animal, bent on the total destruction of everything that walked, breathed, and had fresh blood.

But what I sensed this time was not that out-of-control brute. He was directing a large number of vampires with his mind. As if they were trained guard dogs, they carried out his every direction. That was not the sign of a man out of control. He was very much in control and very much in command of all his faculties.

It was when I realized the entirety of the attack was happening in my home that I lost my composure. It was the moment I saw him feeding on my wife—my immortal love—when I became the deadliest vampire in the world. He felt the change in the air after I tossed him against the wall. But when he heard my voice, he knew he was a dead man walking in more than one way.

He used Alea as a diversion, but he didn't have a clue I'd already decided to wait to kill him later. My Alea always comes first, but she wasn't the only reason I let him leave with his head still attached to his body.

I'm going to kill him slowly.

I plan to take my time with his demise.

He doesn't get off easy for what he's done. He doesn't have the luxury of a quick death waiting for him. He will watch everyone who matters to him die first while he sits helpless and listens to their pleas. He'll have every scream and cry of his clan ringing in his ears when I finally relieve him of that fucking crazy head on his shoulders.

Like the coward he is, he left his perch outside my window while I held my wife's lifeless body to mine. As I cradled her like a child in my arms. While I cried like a baby over my loss. I couldn't hear her heartbeat any longer—not even a faint blip. All that mattered to me in the world was gone. A vampire only has one immortal love in an eternity, never to be replaced, even if one dies.

Eternity is such an abstract term, and until a full century has passed, the true meaning doesn't begin to reveal itself. Because of Ramses's actions, I'd spend an eternity loving a woman I'd never see again, never hold in my arms, never make love to again. All that he took from me could never be replaced. Or forgotten.

Or forgiven.

"Slade, we may still be able to save her," Thomas said in between my sobs.

"Her heart has already stopped," I countered, afraid to hope.

"I met a doctor who has worked with patients who appeared to be dead from blood loss. He used a tube with needles on both ends. He stuck one end in his arm and the other end in the patient's arm.

He gave her his blood, and it saved her. It's worth a try."

Thomas rushed through the house and gathered the supplies he needed. They weren't exactly standard medical supplies, but if they worked, I didn't care what it took. He inserted one needle into my vein, and I watched my vampire-tainted blood crawl through the tube and flow into Alea's arm. Thomas massaged her arm, pushing my blood through her veins. I held my end of the tube high so gravity would force my blood into her body while Thomas mimicked the actions he'd seen the doctor perform.

"The way he described it sounds like the opposite of what we do," he explained, trying to keep me focused. "As we drain blood from a body, the heart slows until it stops. The more blood we get in her, the more the heart should start to pick up. That was his theory anyway."

I'd give her all of my blood if it would bring her back to me. But I also knew it would change her. If it worked, if it saved her, she'd be a vampire before we were ready to make the change. But I'd gladly take her any way I could have her.

After several long seconds, I heard the most beautiful sound in the world. It wasn't her heart beating—any blood that came from my body would make sure of that. But it was the sound of her tissues and organs filling with the instant healing power a vampire's blood provides.

The change a human goes through once infected with vampire blood begins to occur instantly. It's painful to experience. Human traits change over to vampire traits, and the result is a thorough destruction of almost everything that makes up a human's body. Fangs replace normal teeth. Internal organs undergo complete overhauls to accept foreign blood. All the internal changes lead to the external changes.

I was thankful Alea was unconscious while the most painful parts occurred. I was elated when she opened her eyes again, and they searched for me as her brain adjusted to her new eyesight. When the blurriness cleared and she recognized me, her beautiful smile covered her face.

"Slade, you saved me."

"You saved me, my love. I can't live an eternity without you now. So there's no way I could let you leave me."

A pain hit her abdomen, and she drew up in a ball from the swift and severe force of it.

"You need to feed, sweetheart. It's important for a new vampire to feed quickly and often for the first few days while you're building your strength. Dying takes a lot out of you."

She flashed a small smile my way, even through the pain she felt. "Okay, my love. Let's go find Ramses, and I'll feed on him until he's no more than a shriveled pile of bones."

"I love your feistiness. But you're not strong enough to take him on yet. Let's go find you a nice, defenseless mortal first. Ramses will get his comeuppance soon enough."

After helping her to her feet, I turned to Thomas, and for the first time in our immortal friendship, I hugged him with all my might. He chuckled and coughed mockingly.

"I can't breathe, Slade," he joked.

"We don't breathe at all, Thomas," I replied. "Thank you, my friend." I released him and stepped back.

"No thanks needed. You would've been hell to live with for all eternity without this pretty little lady to keep your grumpy moods in check."

"You tried to warn me about Ramses, but I wouldn't listen. I was sure you'd misinterpreted your vision. I won't make that mistake again."

"I didn't see this, Slade. I saw the clan he was building and treating them as his own personal army of henchmen. But this attack was hidden from my sight."

"It's not your fault, so lose the guilty tone. You saved Alea's life. She's still with me because of you. Now I'm going to take my wife out for a drink to celebrate. Don't wait up for us."

Alea and I talked about the events of the night as we strolled the darkened streets together. She remembered most of it, but by the time I'd tossed Ramses across the room, she had already passed out. I filled her in on the details she missed—right down to the silver-bladed knife I held to Ramses's throat. The blade was so sharp, just a touch against his throat split his skin.

That was when I decided to give him a slow, torturous death. Alea's devious side came out with full force when I clued her in on my plans. My feisty little wife will make a formidable vampire. Beheading a vampire with a pure silver blade is the only way to kill him. She has plans to chop off more interesting protruding body parts first.

When we reached the area where her parents live, we both stopped walking at the same time. With her change, our thoughts and feelings are much more in tune and shared. We both felt something terrible had happened to them. In fact, we knew before we confirmed it with our own eyes. We knew Ramses had already been there and killed her family.

Once inside the house, her whole body shook from a mixture of desolation and wrath. Upon seeing her parents, her tears of pain turned to wails of anguish. All I could do was hold her in my arms, reassuring her as best I could, until she had no more tears to shed. The man in me, the one who worships at her feet, wanted to take the pain from her. The monster in me, the one who always lurks in the shadows, wanted to repay Ramses for it one hundredfold.

"Is this normal for vampires to kill the extended families of other vampires?" she asked quietly while staring at her mother's lifeless body, when she was finally able to speak again.

"No. Even among vampires, this is off-limits. It's a completely disrespectful act—an intentional act by someone who knows your family is my family."

"I just nursed her back to health. She wanted us to come over for tea and stay for dinner when you returned from your trip." The sadness dripped from her words and her tone. She will feel this loss for many years to come.

Alea Barnett, 1790

When Slade first told me he was a vampire, and I knew he'd eventually change me, I couldn't bring myself to even consider feeding on people by drinking their blood. Besides the fact it made me nauseous even to think of ingesting blood, killing someone was so far beyond my realm of comprehension I never even gave it much thought.

After feeling the stabbing, searing pain of hunger pangs, the mere thought of it no longer repulsed me. It excited me and made me feel everything related to elation all at once. I felt more alive than I'd ever felt when I was actually still considered as one of the living.

All of my senses were on high alert and extra-enhanced. Sight, smell, touch, taste, hearing—it was all so much better than before. I felt stronger, too, even though Slade basically told me I was still too weak to confront Ramses.

"Slade, how will I know whom to feed on and whom not to?" I wanted to know everything about my new life, but food was high on my list of importance.

"You'll know. You won't even have to ask."

We reached the part of the city that never slept, where the nightlife I was never allowed to partake in before my death occurred in secret basement hideouts. Slade guided me expertly through the maze of hallways and doors until we reached the entrance to one of the underground clubs. The band played, the patrons drank sweet wine or hard liquor and danced, while men bought ladies of the night for a quick rendezvous in one of the dark corners of the club.

When I caught the scent of a young lady walking by me, Slade's words made complete sense. I knew she was the one who would be my first kill. Slade knew, too. He smiled knowingly and guided me behind her, falling in line with her footsteps. The man she was hanging all over couldn't wait to get her in one of the private back rooms so he could fuck her.

Part of me wanted to wait and watch.

But I was far too hungry to do that. When they reached the dark corner of the back room, the man locked the door behind him. Slade chuckled lightly and turned to me.

"Concentrate on moving through that door without opening it. Change into a puff of smoke and walk through it."

I focused as he instructed and walked effortlessly through the thick, wood door. Slade followed immediately behind me. We stood in the nearly pitch-black room and watched the couple undress each other as easily as if we were in a brightly lit room. Then I understood my vampire eyes could see better in the darkest night than during the brightest day.

She dropped to her knees and drew his cock deep into her mouth. Her head bobbed back and forth while his hips rocked into her, matching her rhythm. His hands gripped her hair, holding her head still while his hips picked up speed. She moaned, loving the feel of his slick cock sliding against her tongue and hitting the back of her throat.

My gaze drifted up to meet Slade's, and I saw in his eyes what must have been a mirror of my own thoughts. Desire, for each other. Hunger, for their blood. Excitement, for the thrill of the hunt. Thirst, for the anticipation of the kill.

"Take her now, my love. She's ready. Her blood will taste sweet."

I moved from the door to where my victim knelt in less than a blink of an eye. Confusion and fear marred her features. Her heart raced and sounded as loud as stampeding horses. I opened my mouth, preparing to feed as I lifted her to her feet with one finger, and my fangs extended on their own.

Before her screams could fill the room, I'd drained half of her blood and Slade fed on her companion. When I'd taken all she had to offer, I watched her slump to the floor, her breathing slow and labored, her heart barely beating. Slade's hands covered my cheeks, and he drew me in for a searing hot kiss. The taste of our victims' blood lingered on our tongues and mixed with our own essences, creating a new and exciting flavor.

While they drifted into unconsciousness and eventually death, my husband and I finished what they'd originally entered this room to do. I assumed her position on my knees in front of him and guided his cock to my lips. I ran my tongue around the head and up and down the length of his shaft.

With our clothes shed, his fingers found my pussy already swollen with desire before he thrust them deeply inside me. "Alea, you have no idea what it does to me to know how much you want me."

"I do want you. I want all of you."

He turned me around and pushed on my upper back until I bent all the way forward. "I'm going to give you all you can fucking take of me, and then I'll give you even more. Every day of your immortal life."

My lips were poised to respond, but he slammed into me from behind before I could mutter a single word. The sensation of him filling me to the point of painful stretching was the most deliciously erotic sensation. In an instant, I realized just how much he'd held back when I was still mortal. Now that he could lose control and not risk hurting me, his thrusts became more powerful and his drive took him deeper inside me.

Wave after wave, his hips surged into me and my pleasure sensors soon overloaded. With his name on my lips, I tumbled over the edge of ecstasy and into the arms of complete bliss, and he immediately followed.

An eternity of this with him will never be long enough.

After we left the underground club, we walked and talked about the events of the night and how we'd handle what Ramses had done to us.

"I didn't want this for you so soon," Slade said, his tone full of remorse. "I had to change you to save you, though."

"I'm glad you did, Slade. I don't regret it or hold you responsible at all. Our eternity as a married vampire couple may have started a few years ahead of your plan, but all that matters is we're together."

My words seemed to help him accept what he'd been forced to do. What Ramses had forced him to do. But I meant it—there's nothing I wouldn't do to ensure we stayed together.

Finding what Ramses had done to my parents was beyond devastating. I don't even know of a word that describes the hurt, anger, and betrayal I felt. Seeing them left not one shred of doubt in my mind that his sole intention was to kill me too. He wasn't just after blood—his acts of treachery were very personal and meticulous.

He struck at my parents' house first from what we could tell from the condition of their bodies. The hardening that occurs in the deceased had already set in. As I stood there, I remembered when my grandfather died. It took a few hours for that to happen to his body, but it scared me when it did. My father patiently explained the same thing had scared him as a child when his own grandfather died. I suddenly realized I'd never hear my parents share stories from their childhoods again. I'd never hear their voices, feel their embrace, or tell them how much I loved and appreciated them.

As if he read my thoughts, Slade wrapped his arms around my waist from behind, rested his chin on my shoulder, and quietly comforted me. "I feel the heartbreak and grief radiating from you. I'd bear the full burden of your pain if I could. What can I do to help? Say the word, and it's yours."

His words struck another chord in me, bringing another conversation to the forefront of my mind. Slade and I can never have children of our own, and though I would've chosen him regardless, I was suddenly relieved it was impossible. I would never want my children to feel the soul-slashing torment of losing a parent.

"There is one thing you can do, Slade," I replied after several silent moments. "Make me strong enough to kill Ramses myself."

The way his entire body tensed behind me spoke volumes before he said a word in response. Our connection was strong before he changed me, but now it felt like we were one person split into two bodies. The way he felt my pain—I felt what he felt.

Hesitation. Concern. Doubt. Empathy. Rage. Regret.

It's strange to think vampires have all the same feelings humans have, when all the fictional stories cast such a blackness around them. Now that I can speak from firsthand experience on the subject, I'd say it's actually the complete opposite. As with our enhanced senses, our feelings seem to be multiplied as well.

Slade dropped his forehead on my shoulder and shook his head from side to side while he released a deep sigh. My grief was far too great to appreciate the irony of that act at the time. The deep sigh—a human reaction that concedes defeat to do something we'd rather not do, while knowing the alternative would be worse.

Acceptance of the lesser of two evils.

That somewhat amuses me—now, at least, as I write this entry in my journal. Am I the lesser of two evils?

"You're worried I won't be able to stand against him," I spoke his thoughts for him. "That Ramses will kill me and take me from you. You're angry with him for what he's done, and part of you wants to kill him yourself. But he's your brother, so another part of you doesn't want it at all. I understand why, and I can't blame you for being conflicted.

"But he took my family from me, then tried to kill me. I remember the things he said to me when I thought he was you. He must have had a part in Sean's death for him to know about that. The last thing I want is to hurt you, but I can't let him live."

"What things did he say to you? I came in and found him feeding on you."

I knew when I repeated Ramses's words, Slade would be furious and hurt at the same time. Though I suspected his rage would burn hot enough to eclipse the pain of his brother's betrayal. In a way, I hated to tell him any of it because he'd been with Ramses for over a century before I came along. Ramses is his brother in more than one way—by family name and by vampire clan. Losing that connection would be just as difficult as what I'm experiencing with the loss of my parents.

What I didn't expect was the quiet and composed demeanor Slade displayed when I finished detailing the exchange prior to his arrival. I expected to feel his muscles tense and for his body to become rigid. But that didn't happen. I thought he'd yell, break things, and curse. But he remained eerily silent. I pictured him bolting from the house on his own quest to find and kill Ramses, yet he remained in place.

But when he gently turned me around to face him, his appearance shocked me. The love and warmth I've always seen and felt in his eyes was gone. In fact, had I not known my husband the way I do, I wouldn't have believed he was the same man. The icy blue hue of his eyes matched the layer of frost that covered his heart before a flash of deep red flared in them. His vampiric features were more defined than when we fed just a short time before. They were fierce, dark, and inherently lethal.

The timbre of his voice was naturally deeper when his true nature was displayed. But the voice that emanated from my love stunned me with its underlying ferocity. He'd long surpassed upset, mad, angry, furious, or enraged—and welcomed the burn of pure, bitter hatred with his arms wide open.

"I will teach you everything you need to know.

I will make you the most feared vampire in the history of vampires. But his head is mine. You can burn his body one piece at a time if you want.

"For your loss, I wanted to give you the pleasure of doing it yourself. Hearing what he said to you changed my mind, though. I have to live an eternity knowing what he said to you, but it's even worse knowing that you, my love, have to live with an eternity of knowing I wasn't there to protect you. That was intentional on his part, attacking when I was away. I can't erase it from your memory, but I will make him wish he'd never been born."

Chapter Ten

Ramses Barnett, 1790

As I write this, I feel as if I have two completely different people warring inside my head. What I did to my brother, the one who's been by my side and helped me at every turn, was unforgivable even in the cutthroat vampire world. That kind of betrayal just isn't tolerated against family or friends. If I somehow escape the wrath of my brother's revenge, other vampires will step up and relieve me of my head for him.

No one wants a traitor in their midst.

They won't care how terrible I feel for the pain I've caused him. They won't listen to my pitiful excuses for what pushed me to do that to him and his wife. And his household servants. And her parents.

I'm so fucked—and not in the way I prefer.

Here's where I have to face my own demons. The ones I hide from the world—even my brother. My faults I can barely admit to myself, much less to anyone else. The characteristics that make me who I am are the very things I'm most ashamed of.

He's my younger brother, but he's always been the more mature one.

He was supposed to look up to me, but I've always admired him.

He was supposed to learn from me, but he has taught me more than I've ever taught him.

He was supposed to emulate me.

I wasn't supposed to want to be him.

I wasn't supposed to want his life.

I shouldn't envy my brother and his success, his drive, or his wife.

So there it is—well, part of it anyway. Part of what propels me to insanity. My feelings of being inferior and how I constantly feel the need to prove my worth. The more reckless I became, the more I had to brag about. The more others were afraid of me, the more powerful it made me feel.

I love my brother.

And I hate him.

Because I'm not him, and I desperately want to be.

To make sense, I suppose I should start at the beginning and confess to the things I've been doing behind his back. The secret deals and meetings he never knew anything about. The secret plans I've crafted and built a team to help me execute every facet.

My team. My army.

My vampire army.

I originally started building it for both Slade and me. I'd planned to speak to him about it and convince him it was the best course of action, but it never seemed to be the right time to broach the subject.

By the time I decided to move ahead with it, my idea had taken on a life of its own. And once I get fixated on something, it's impossible for me to move on from it. It becomes my obsession.

Thomas has always been an excellent assistant and can run our business almost as well as we can. But for this task, I needed someone else—someone who could keep my secrets until I was ready to reveal them. I needed someone Slade didn't know and therefore couldn't control with his powers.

That's why I found Patrick and befriended him. It didn't take long to reveal myself to him and show him what I could do. He immediately wanted in, so I turned him, and he helped me build a powerful new clan. Patrick managed my secret house while I traveled. My obsession with Alea threatened our business—and my ability to be in the same city with her and not drink her dry was completely lost.

The more I resisted the urge, the more it became unbearable. With her family's societal standing, I would've ruined Slade and myself professionally and personally, along with revealing our kind to the new world.

So I left, and Patrick stayed with Richelle and Corinne while I was away...while I went back to England to ruin Alea's family's name along with her precious friend Sean and his family. After Clarence forbade her from seeing me again, my anger ran through me like a rampant fever. The more I dwelt on it, the more it consumed me and pushed me to make the rash decisions that brought me to the state I'm in now.

Sean was the first in a long line of my regrets. I knew it would hurt Alea and make her feel responsible for his demise. That day is forever seared in my memory.

"Hello, I'm Ramses Barnett. You are?" I asked as I approached the handsome young man at the pub.

"Sean Naster. Pleasure to meet you." He replied with the politeness expected of his station, but he wasn't sure of my intentions.

I ignored his unease and continued speaking as if I were a long-lost friend. He visibly relaxed and soon engaged in conversation. We spoke of the usual boring pleasantries as we became more and more acquainted. He told me all about his family and their estate. I shared similar stories of my fake family. He excitedly shared the plans his father had for turning the family business over to him, and I voluntarily shared my business experience and offers of advice and help should he need it.

Eventually, we worked our way around to the very subject I was there to speak to him about.

"Which of these lovely ladies around here has caught your affections?" I asked, flashing my warm and friendly smile.

He hesitated and appeared genuinely uncomfortable. He nervously cleared his throat before answering. "My betrothed moved to America and annulled our engagement. I'm in between love interests at the moment, I'm afraid."

"That had to smart. My apologies for summoning such a painful memory."

"It did hurt, actually. We were good friends before our parents arranged our marriage. She was the best friend I've ever had, and I miss her companionship."

"You weren't in love with her, though. Were you?"

"No, I suppose I wasn't. I loved her as a friend, but neither of us was too keen on marrying the other. The friendship was solid, but the deeper feelings were not there."

"I've found it's better to stay unattached for as long as possible. It's much more fun that way.

You're much too young to be married now anyway."

"Not according to my mother," he chuckled. "She's been inconsolable since the wedding was canceled."

"Sounds like you could use a long night out with the guys to have a little fun and get away from the pressures of home. I'm sure you have friends who could throw you a fun anti-stag party."

I watched while my suggestion took root in his mind and became its own living entity. It was the perfect excuse he needed to plan a getaway with his secret lover. His parents would understand his need to escape for a few days with his friends and forget how he was humiliated after losing his fiancée via letter. He could make up any story he wanted about their adventure, and his parents would never know the difference. It was finally his chance to spend an entire night, or several, with his friend.

"You're right. That's exactly what I need—to get away and have some fun while I'm still young and single. A night in London, tracking from one pub to the next, checking out the ladies, without responsibilities or a mother obsessing over me, sounds like heaven." He smiled the first genuine smile of the night as his mind plotted out the details.

"You know, you should go this weekend. The London Festival starts tomorrow, and it should be a howling good time," I suggested and waited for him to catch up.

A.D. Justice

"The London Festival? You mean the masquerade party that lasts a fortnight? The one that makes the whole city buzz with excitement? With festivities on every street corner? You are absolutely brilliant. I'm ready to make plans to leave tonight."

That was my plan—to encourage him just enough that my intentions weren't obvious. A covert suggestion to persuade him, tempt him, and ultimately trap him. He played right into my hands.

Young Sean left the pub in a hurry when I mentioned how difficult it would be to secure appropriate accommodations should he dally too long. From there, it was only a matter of time before his secrets were revealed.

The weekend brought the revelers to the streets of downtown London. The gypsies danced in the streets and performed their tricks. The band played, and the music carried in the air, echoed off the buildings, and vibrated in the veins of every mortal. The fourteen-day-long party provided the ultimate feast and an unparalleled cover to hide the number of missing humans.

I followed Sean and his young lover through the streets, hidden in the masses of people. They never knew I watched while they ate, drank, danced, and lived as though they didn't have a care in the world. They were just two young men in the city to enjoy the same festival many other best friends were. The first couple of nights, they were extra careful with their interactions—avoiding personal contact and any appearance they were a couple.

After nights of alcohol and being away from the watchful eyes of their parents, the pair became less careful, bolder, and lost their inhibitions. That was my sign. When they retired to their rented room for the night, I watched through the window until they embraced each other and fused their lips together. Within seconds, I'd found a constable walking on the street below and reported their crime of unnatural acts. As a concerned citizen, it was my duty to inform the officer of such acts occurring in the room next to mine. The constable was all too willing to oblige me and investigate my concerns.

When he burst through the door without warning and caught them in the act, there was no denying their crime. With all the eyewitnesses watching from the hallway, there was no need for a trial. To save his family the public shaming and embarrassment, Sean asked for a speedy sentence. Before his parents could arrive from the countryside outside London proper, Sean was hung as punishment for his crime.

And all I could do was think about rushing back to America to tell Alea myself. So I could see her face. So I could feel her anger and pain roll off her and crash into me, fueling my hatred, feeding my anger, cocooning me in my obsession.

Distance gives perspective. It seems hypocritical of a vampire to ruminate over feeling guilty for causing a man to die. Yet, here I sit, regretting my vampiric flight across the ocean to London. I regret setting such a bright young man on his path to destruction. I regret using him as a pawn in my deadly game. I regret that he chose a quick death, preserving his honor and nobility while sparing his family from a long, drawn-out process.

I regret not having that same noble and honorable nature in me.

As evident from the acts I carried out upon my return to New York. Alea's parents. Alea herself—my brother's wife. My sister by law—human law and vampire alike. But it's really worse than breaking a rule my kind cannot forgive.

I broke my bond to my brother. I betrayed his love and his trust. I've created an enemy out of the worst person I could've possibly chosen. His strength is by far the greatest I've ever seen, but when he saw me feeding on Alea, it became more.

More focused.

More ambitious.

More furious.

More lethal.

He'll come for me, but I don't want to fight him. He would no doubt win a fair fight—but I don't want to kill my brother, not by tricks or ruses. I don't want to hurt my brother, any more than I already have, at least. At the same time, I don't want to die, especially before I've had an opportunity to make amends. Somehow.

In the meantime, I find my options limited, and the only acceptable choice really isn't acceptable at all. I'm forced to increase the numbers of my clan, to move ahead with ideas for new businesses, and to add to my secret stash of humans to feed on in private quarters. Though it may be akin to humans eating the same food every day without variety, my plan at least gives us shelter and keeps us hidden when we need it.

And I will most certainly need the shelter for quite a while. This city has become my home, and I don't want to leave. There must be a way to work this out to our mutual benefit.

Tonight, I moved through the streets and kept to the darkness, checked around corners, and watched over my shoulder, waiting for my brother to appear out of thin air and cut off my head. My clan is out increasing our numbers a few at a time, but I'm going stir-crazy not being part of the action.

Plus, the novelty of Richelle and Corinne turned to monotony, so I gave them to Patrick. I went out on the prowl for more to join them and found two more who fit my tastes. They don't have the hold Alea has over me. If I could find someone like her, a woman whose blood makes mine boil with desire, I would never become bored. I'd never tire of her. I'd never need another.

She would be my immortal love.

Patrick came back from the hunt tonight and reported to me, as per protocol.

"We added fifteen more tonight. They're in the basement of The Sanctuary undergoing their immortal births. They should be ready to swear allegiance to our clan in a couple of days. We'll have plenty of vampires to protect you once the others we brought in are ready in the morning."

"Thanks for the good news on the numbers. But don't put them in front of me if Slade comes after me. Or, more accurately, *when* he comes for me. They won't be able to stand against him. Take my word for it."

Slade Barnett, 1790

My wife is learning her new life so fast, I'm convinced she was born to be a vampire. My shy, timid little proper lady was born to be fierce, fearless, and confident. There's always the possibility that her hatred and thirst for revenge are driving her more than anything else. She's dead set on being the one who takes Ramses down. At the rate she's excelling, I can hardly doubt it will be her.

But she also understands my position. She respects my request as I respect hers. First, as well as she's doing, as strong as she is mentally and physically, his years of developing skills and strength would completely eclipse her measly few weeks of training. Second, my brother betrayed me by feeding on my wife. It is my right and duty as a man and a husband to obliterate him.

It's the noble and honorable thing to do.

Thomas and I have been watching Ramses and his clan's movements, and they don't have a clue. The number of people missing has started to raise too many alarms. Illustrations of missing loved ones are in every shop window and being handed out on every street corner with the newspapers. It's only a matter of time before an observant citizen recognizes one of the faces. Before I put an end to Ramses, we need to know what he and his clan are planning.

I've put all of my focus into training Alea, and she has willingly accepted every word. She is my only escape, and she keeps the monster inside me at bay. I felt him trying to escape the night I almost lost my world. It was all I could do to prevent him from taking over and destroying everything in sight. As a matter of fact, I don't think I would have gotten him under control if Ramses hadn't mentioned her at the moment he did.

Knowing that darkness lives inside me is one reason why I've been overly patient with Ramses during his episodes. I've never told him about my own demon because he would only use it as an excuse to dismiss his madness. Ramses is weak. Had he channeled his inner strength, he would be so much more than he is. He could harness that incredible power and make it work for him, make it bend to his will instead of him always bending to it.

Only Thomas knows about what I keep suppressed inside me. He had a vision once where it got loose, and the devastation was unreal. Even as hardened and experienced as Thomas is, he was shaken up from everything he saw. He was cautious when he approached me, but he was also direct. I've heeded his warning since that day, and I've attempted to keep Ramses in a steady state as well.

But that night, I wanted to let him out. I wanted to annihilate Ramses. Every time I've seen him on our spying missions since then, Thomas whispered Alea's name to me to save us all from whatever this dark force inside me is. I wish I knew what it was, what it would do if it were loosed. All I know for certain is Alea's presence calms it. It doesn't want to lose her any more than I do.

I was lost in my musings, deep in reflective thought, when my love surprised me.

"You are a wonderful teacher, Slade." She complimented me as she straddled my lap. I love when she gets frisky and excited. It's the ultimate turn-on when my woman demands sex from me.

"You're an even better student," I replied and slid my hands under her shirt. My fingers glided against her skin as I wrapped them around her waist. "Is there something else you'd like me to teach you tonight?"

"Maybe you can try to teach me that trick you do with your tongue. I don't think I quite figured it out last time."

"It would definitely be my pleasure to give you another demonstration of my tongue-flicking skills. I seem to remember you enjoyed dreaming of that before we married. Every night, in fact."

"Yes, my dreams." She cut her eyes at me sideways in a mock glare. "That's one thing you haven't taught me yet. How did you do that?"

I couldn't help but grin at her in reply. "Every vampire has different gifts. They develop and strengthen over time. One of my gifts is the ability to control people's dreams. In your case, I made them all about me.

"The many times I was actually in your bed with you, I had you under my trance. I can gently persuade people to do what I want them to do. It's more difficult with the strong-willed, but weak-minded people are easy to control."

"Are you saying I'm weak-minded?"

"Not at all. You remembered every time, didn't you?"

"Yes. At the time, I thought they were all dreams. But now that you mention it, there were some that felt different from the others. They felt more real. Now I know they were real."

"It took all of my focus to keep you in a semi-trance state. You started slipping out of it when my mind strayed to more distracting things. Like how good you tasted when I flicked my tongue against your clit."

"Take me to our bedroom and attempt your trance on me now, Mr. Barnett. Your wife is waiting."

When my wife openly asks for a thorough fucking, the one thing she'll never do is wait for it.

Chapter Eleven

Alea Barnett, December 1790

Snowflakes falling in New York on Christmas Eve night is a beautiful sight. I could sit and watch them for hours now because I can see each individual snowflake. The tiny designs of crystals are different in every one—but they're all equally beautiful.

They also distract me from the madness of our current world. I haven't journaled in quite a while because we've all been so busy.

The reality of my life is so surreal it's difficult to fathom. A short nine months ago, I embarked on an adventure with my parents by coming to America. In that brief time, everything has changed, including me. Especially me. My family was slaughtered by my brother-in-law, and now we're in the throes of a major clan war. The docile wallflower I once was is dead and long gone. The prim and proper debutante my parents raised me to be has been replaced by a sinister assassin with no qualms about taking a life to prolong mine.

Slade has trained me to be a stealthy killer—lethal in every way. My powers showed up quickly after my birth. Slade passed some of his gifts on to me, and since he shares a bloodline with Ramses, apparently that means I get a dose of his gifts as well. The combination of talents has resulted in a unique outcome for me.

Slade's ability to influence people and enter their dreams, combined with Ramses's ability to read minds, gave me the ability to completely control others for short periods. I should amend that to say I can control those who are weaker. Every day, I practice on Slade since he's the strongest vampire I know. Once I have a slight hold over him, I'll know I'm ready to face Ramses.

Thomas refuses to let me practice on him anymore after our last training test.

"Get out of my head, Alea," he warned. "I can feel you roaming around in there."

"What have you been doing, Thomas?" I asked, quirking one brow upward.

"I don't know what you mean." He denied my insinuation, but his dubious expression said otherwise.

"You've been creating a larger clan for quite a while now, haven't you?"

"That's enough practicing for today." His tone was curt and abrupt, the complete opposite of his usual demeanor.

"Thomas, I didn't mean to imply you've done anything wrong."

He stopped just short of reaching the doorway and turned slowly to face me. "I know you didn't," he replied with a softer tone. "It's true. I have been building Slade's clan, but only as a means to defend ourselves.

"I told Slade some time ago Ramses would do this—he'd turn on us. If we weren't prepared, we'd all be slaughtered. Ramses is building his clan for far more nefarious reasons than mine. He's clearly unstable, but his plans for humans and clan members alike are too dangerous for our kind."

He stopped speaking and looked at me thoughtfully. His eyes crinkled in the corners and narrowed to mere slits.

"What is it?" I asked.

"How did you know that? I wasn't even thinking about it, so it couldn't be because you read my mind."

"I'm beginning to be able to access memories, too. It's odd. Sometimes I can't tell immediately whether it's a current thought or an old memory."

"You've inherited some powerful gifts. You'll make one terrifying vampire when you reach full strength. I'm glad you're on my team."

"Do you see my future?" I was genuinely interested in what Thomas saw for me, what I could look forward to in my new life.

"Not a vision like I normally see. But there's a strong air about you that screams greatness. It's a force that surrounds you and draws others to you."

I laughed with no humor in my tone. "Is that why Ramses was so drawn to me? Is that why he killed my family? Is that why he tried to kill me— because he was drawn to my invisible force?"

One side of his mouth lifted, amused by my sarcastic reply. "No, but I am surprised you haven't worked that out yet. You are quite intelligent."

"Tell me why." He definitely had my full attention. An explanation of why all this lunacy has occurred could help settle the guilt that has built up inside me. Guilt that I encouraged any of this by encouraging Ramses's advances before I met Slade.

"Slade explained you're his immortal love, correct?"

"Yes, he told me every vampire only has one immortal love for eternity. And it's a miracle when they actually find each other."

"That's right. Since Slade and Ramses shared a mortal bloodline as well as an immortal one, it was only natural for Ramses to feel an intense attraction to you. That wouldn't make him do everything he did, though. All of that is on Ramses and Ramses alone.

"What he would've felt toward you, had he been a normal vampire, would be possessive and protective, more like an older brother would toward his sister."

"What do you mean by 'a normal vampire'? How is he not a normal vampire?"

"Ramses has always had difficulties with controlling his impulses. His possessiveness of you turned into an obsession and made his insanity worse."

"He never seemed insane to me when he attended dinners at my father's table."

"He has moments of clarity. Slade was able to keep much of Ramses's illness under control when he was around. But he couldn't be his nanny every moment. Ramses's madness knows no bounds when it gets out of control. He's also always been envious of Slade, so seeing you with his archnemesis was just too much for him.

"His immortal obsession is married to his immortal nemesis. He both loves and hates his brother, just as he loves and hates himself. It's a bad situation all the way around. You were caught in the middle of it, but it's in no way your fault."

"I appreciate your kind words and reassurance, Thomas. Also the insight as to why Ramses behaves the way he does. I would pity him if I weren't filled with complete and utter contempt for him."

Thomas nodded, his facial expression conveying empathy, but his thoughts strayed to regret and sadness. "Take care of your feelings, Alea."

He left me with that ominous warning and no further explanation. Although, I'm afraid I do know exactly what he meant, and it concerns me. If the mad illness came from the original Barnett bloodline and was enhanced from the vampire who turned both brothers, does that mean I'm next in line since that same blood turned me?

I didn't have time to dwell on that thought for long before Slade came in with dried blood on his face and clothes. His eyebrows were drawn down tight, his lips formed a thin line, and his jaw was rigid. He paced back and forth in a barely managed fit of anger. His footsteps fell hard on the wood floor and echoed throughout the house from the force. Whatever happened wasn't good, and from the way his face was contorted in anger, it also wasn't over.

"Slade." I approached him with caution. Not that I think he would ever hurt me, but I could sense from his manner it wouldn't take much to incite his fury. "Talk to me. Tell me what happened. Let me help."

His pacing halted, and his hands curled into fists. "Give me a moment." He managed to keep his tone neutral, but a flash of red flickered in his eyes.

It only lasted a fraction of a second, but I know what I saw. What concerned me the most about the whole situation wasn't the odd color in his eyes or his intense anger or even his refusal to tell me what had happened. It was the sinking feeling in my chest...because I couldn't feel what he felt anymore. For the first time since the night we met, I couldn't feel our connection.

Slade Barnett, 1790

The main objective I have in mind when I set out on my daily quest is to locate Ramses and discover his true intentions. His clan's true intentions. His members are not as clever and stealthy as they think they are. He has too many new, inexperienced changelings who don't know how to control their hunger or how to blend in with the humans. They stick out like a sore thumb, attracting unnecessary attention at every turn. So far, their juvenile antics have occurred late at night when the residential streets are mostly vacant.

The last few times I've been out on my spy missions, I've noticed a distinct change in their behavior. One that's more concerning to me for our overall survival. They're taking humans off the street—snatching them and flying away with the human in their grasp. Their lair must be nearby, at least close enough to take their captives without raising alarms from screams and protests.

So I've waited and watched. I've spent hours of my time awaiting the perfect opportunity. Finally, tonight, it happened. One of the young vampires grabbed a woman, but he hadn't yet gained enough strength to fly away at full speed, and I was close enough to follow him back to their hiding place without being detected. Novice move on his part, really. There's no way Ramses or I would've made such foolish mistakes when we were young vampires, which concerns me even more that Ramses is allowing it to happen with his clan now. I followed the young one inside the three-story building, moving through the corridors with ease.

It was there I realized how badly the madness has claimed my brother and how far he was willing to take it.

Locked in cages in the cold, damp dungeon was one human after the other. The missing posters that littered the city held the faces of most of the people living in the deplorable conditions of Ramses's hideout. A deep, dark basement underneath a house that sat barely outside the city held the power to reveal all vampires, putting our entire race in jeopardy, and bringing the wrath of all humans down on top of us. These humans weren't being turned. They weren't given the option of immortality. They were all so young. Many of them were much too young to be vampires. But they were all held as prisoners and repeatedly fed upon.

If any other vampire found out about this, we'd all be killed. All the vampires in the city would be eliminated on principle and an abundance of caution.

"What are you doing, brother?" I asked aloud as I strode through the rows upon rows of caged humans.

"I'm doing what you never had the foresight to do," he replied from behind me. "Or the balls."

When I turned to face him, his smug grin disappeared as I retorted. "My balls are bigger than yours. Always have been. Always will be."

Our eyes connected and a stare-down ensued, neither of us willing to be the first to yield. The vision of his fangs in Alea's neck sprang to my mind, and my rage increased tenfold, filling me up inside. The longer I stood there, the more it built inside me until it erupted like a raging volcano that would consume everything in its path. Swift determination guided my feet, and shameless reprisal directed my hands. My fingers curled into tight fists, and I took pleasure in repeatedly smashing them into his face. Though I knew my blows could cause him no long-term damage, I took great pleasure from every second of it.

Then the volcano erupted, and I felt my control slipping.

The beast that has been trapped inside me

became free, and I felt his power surge within me. Power unlike anything I've ever known pumped in my veins, fortifying my resolve to end this once and for all. To end Ramses. My fist moved toward his face even faster than my normal speed, connecting with his tough vampire skin and leaving increasingly worse marks with each relentless blow. Soon, his blood ran down his face because the swelling and bruising split the skin on his cheek. In the dark recesses of my mind, I knew it would heal within minutes, but that didn't stop me from savoring the sight of his battered face and swollen eyes while I could.

The frightened screams from the caged prisoners brought other members of his clan to the basement. In their rush to determine the origin of the commotion, they didn't take the time to assess their surroundings before charging headlong into the battle. The addition of incensed vampires only further ignited my ferocity and my momentum. To everyone else in the room, Ramses appeared to be flailing about unaided.

"Ramses, what's happening to you?" The horrified expression on one of the younger one's faces almost elicited a laugh from me.

"Tell us what to do!" another yelled, a young boy who had no business being turned.

"Grab him!" Ramses yelled between blows.

"Grab who? There's no one here," the young

boy replied. His eyes were wide open, his head shook from side to side in slow motion, and his steps carried him backward, toward the steps and away from the action.

I felt Ramses's blood splash across my face as it sprayed through the air, droplets falling like rain on the floor, but I continued my unremitting assault.

"My brother." He doubled over as my fist connected with his ribs on his reply. The crack of his bones breaking echoed throughout the enormous room.

My hand wrapped around the handle of my knife hidden just under my jacket. I moved like the wind, invisible and quick, when I plunged the knife deep into his chest. It wouldn't kill him, but it would burn like the devil. I stopped moving and held the knife in place, stood eye-to-eye with my brother, and read his thoughts that tore through his mind.

Why are his eyes red?

Is that how he's able to move so fast?

What does he have that I don't?

Why did our maker give him the best gifts instead of me?

His clan members stood as still as statues. Bewilderment masked their faces, and fear of the unknown gripped their wits. When I slid my gaze over to meet theirs, my eyes emblazoned with a blood-red hue, they dropped to their knees and cowered. "Please spare us, Master."

Master?

"Leave. Now." My deeper voice turned my words into a growl that rattled the metal bars on the cages. Within seconds, they disappeared up the steps, leaving me alone with my brother.

"Slade, you can't do this. We're brothers."

His pleas fell on deaf ears.

"You killed Alea's parents. You invaded my house. You killed members of my clan. But worst of all, you fed on my wife." I could see the reflection of my glowing red eyes in his as I twisted the silver blade in his chest. "You are not my brother. You are my enemy, and I obliterate my enemies."

His face was twisted with pain. He grimaced with every slight movement of the blade. The mere touch of it burned him like a sizzling branding iron. "Give me an opportunity to apologize."

"Apologize? Do you honestly think a mere 'I'm sorry I killed your wife' will assuage me? That your promise never to betray me again will appease my thirst for your life?" I lowered my chin and looked at him from under my drawn brows. "After all these years, you must know me better than to believe that."

I withdrew the knife from his chest with controlled movements, taking my time to subject him to as much pain as possible, and held it to his throat. His skin sizzled from the searing quality of pure silver. "I do know you, Slade. You could never do this to me."

I pressed the knife farther into his skin. "You're right," I nodded. Relief and hope filled his eyes. "I couldn't cut your head off and mount it above my fireplace...before you killed my wife. She's my immortal love. When you attacked her, you changed everything. You changed *me*."

"She was your immortal love?"

"She *is*," I stressed the present tense to correct him.

He squeezed his eyes shut, and the gravity of his situation hit him with full force. "What have I done?" he whispered, more to himself than to me.

"You've woken the monster that lives inside me, that's what you've done."

"If there were anything I could do to bring her back, I would do it, Slade. I would give anything to make amends for what I've done..."

"Oh, you will," I assured him. "You will give your immortal life to pay for what you've done."

"I'm afraid I can't allow that, Slade," a familiar voice said from behind me.

When I turned, I couldn't believe my eyes. "Castel? Why are you here?"

"You have to let your brother go, Slade."

"Are you helping him with this?"

He chuckled without a bit of humor. "No, I have no part in any of this," Castel replied. "When I felt the murderous mayhem between you two, I knew

I'd have to show up to stop you."

"How did you know what was happening between us if you're not part of his plan?"

"I made both of you." He shrugged, as if that explained everything. "Release him, Slade. Now."

Though the incredible power inside me still burned strong, I had no choice but to obey him. He's my maker, and he passed on the ability to control others to me. The same gift I use against others was used against me to force my hands to release Ramses.

"Go home, Slade," Castel ordered. "We'll talk soon."

I stormed into our home, the red still burning in my eyes, the monster barely contained from taking out his wrath on anyone and anything around me. As I paced back and forth, Alea's thoughts ranged from confusion to concern for me to disbelief about the whole situation. One of her thoughts I heard loud and clear was how she felt completely disconnected from me.

And she was right.

When the monster was loosed, I wasn't me.

It was only after I returned home and began recounting the events of the night I realized...I had been able to read their minds.

I've never had that gift before, and I don't have it now that my eyes are blue again.

Chapter twelve

Ramses Barnett, 1790

"Castel?" I repeated Slade's question after he'd left. I still couldn't believe our immortal father stood before me. He saved me from certain death at Slade's hands. I knew I'd met my end when Slade's physical strength caused bodily harm to my thick vampire skin. When my blood spattered across his face and the floor, I imagined his smile while slitting my throat before decapitating me. After my traitorous actions, I couldn't blame him for taking his revenge. As brothers, I at last understood the magnitude of my betrayal.

Castel kept his eyes fixed on mine as he walked toward me. He shook his head from side to side, making a *tsking* noise to convey his deep disappointment in me.

"Ramses, what you did to Slade's wife and his home is not forgiven in our world. You know this. You knew it when you did it."

"I did." I couldn't lie to him. There was no point in trying anyway. "I knew. But I couldn't resist Alea. There's something in her blood that makes me crazy."

Castel raised one eyebrow in a wordless challenge.

"Crazier," I amended.

"She's Slade's immortal love. It's only natural you would have a strong connection to her, too."

"It's more than that, Castel. Her blood made me feel alive and out of control. When I tasted it, I thought about keeping her here so I could taste it every day. But my envy and my obsession with her took control of me, and I decided she had to die. Slade will never forgive me for killing Alea, for taking her from him for all eternity."

"You didn't. But there's more to the hold she has on you than simple blood lust."

"Wait. What do you mean I didn't?"

"He found a way to get his vampire blood in her and changed her before it was too late. You're very fortunate he did, too, because I would have to destroy you otherwise. You seem to have found somewhat of a loophole in the laws. Though, if we were to put it to a vote, you'd still lose. Slade would be awarded the right to relieve you of your head.

"However, what you're doing here in this basement is beyond the reach I possess to protect you should others find this. Your prisoners can't be released because there are too many of them. Their stories would be too similar and would prompt a door-to-door manhunt for the lunatic who took them. Most of them are too young to be changed—that would bring more scrutiny from powerful vampires you'd rather not meet.

"You'll have to change the ones you can and kill the ones you can't. Get rid of this and never do this again, Ramses. Don't make me have to come back here again."

With that directive, Castel disappeared before my eyes. Right before my eyes. No vampire has ever done that before. Even with Slade's red-eyed speed, I could feel his presence in the room. Castel was just gone, like a puff of smoke dissipates into the air.

I sank into the nearest chair and digested his words. The revelation that Alea was still around, even as a vampire, was shocking, to say the least. A little fact Slade neglected to mention when he used my face as his personal punching bag and my chest as a carving board. He still has her, mostly intact, yet he intended to kill me over her anyway.

Castel left before I could address the other revelation he dropped on me like a ton of lead. If it's not her blood I crave, regardless of how sweet and tempting it is, then what is it? What does she have that I so desperately need?

I called to my army of changelings to dispose of the feeders we'd amassed. At that one particular location anyway. I diversified my business when Slade and I first parted ways. Just in case of emergencies such as this one. The older captives made a nice addition to our clan numbers, while the younger ones made nice meals for the changelings.

"Send extra soldiers to the other locations to ensure there are no problems. No escapees, no suspicious activity, no reason for anyone to give them a second glance," I ordered my next in command. He assembled dozens of vampires and left to get them into place at my other houses. Business has been good, and I plan to keep it that way for as long as possible.

When night fell again, I chanced a trip to Slade's house. If Alea was still there, I had to see it for myself. I had to feel it for myself. If the madness reappeared, if the obsession returned, I'd have my answer. It was she who made me lose control.

If the obsession was quiet with her being a vampire now, I had no worries.

I watched through the window where I first saw them together. I waited for them to retire to the privacy of their large master bedroom. My fingers gripped the brick window ledge when I heard voices approaching.

There she was. Even more beautiful now than

when she was alive. Even more vibrant than before. Infinitely more irresistible. Castel's warning echoed in my mind, almost as loudly as if he'd spoken the command directly into my ear.

Don't make me have to destroy you.

The warning was clear enough I couldn't question it—or how serious he was that he'd do exactly as he threatened to do.

She had more than a hold on me. It was more than I simply wanted to drink her blood. She was turned, and I wanted her more than ever before. She was immortal, but that in no way lessened my obsession with her. She was a vampire, but what I felt was a physical need for her.

Leave. Right. Now.

I had no choice but to obey Castel's command. Besides knowing it was my final warning, I was wholly incapable of disobeying him. As hard and painful as it was, I left their house and my perch on their window before it was too late for any of us.

How I can find the strength to stay away is up for debate.

One thing I know for sure is I must learn why this is happening. What is it about her that I can't resist, that I'd essentially risk my immortal life to have? I have a strong instinct Castel knows exactly why. I also believe he is keeping the information from me in a deliberate move. It must be a means to keep me away from Alea and Slade.

What he doesn't seem to understand is my body needs her.

I need her.

Alea Barnett, January 1791

I've felt a strange presence following me the last few nights when I've gone out to feed. I've stopped and kept my own thoughts silent so I could focus on hearing what my persistent follower had to say. Though I heard nothing, the power I felt emanating from whoever followed me was potent. The strength exuded no doubt came from an old, powerful being, though for some reason, I couldn't say with any certainty that it was a vampire. I know how other vampires feel when they're close. That wasn't the same feeling I felt.

"I know you're there. Following me. Watching me. But I don't know why. Come out and talk to me."

My words floated across the air in the dark of the night, and I waited patiently for a response. Any response would suffice—a thought, a movement, a spoken word. But there was nothing at all, not even the normal sounds of the city. Everything around me became completely silent, proving my powerful companion was still there.

But for what purpose?

The next time I felt the presence was in the

middle of a blustering, winter day. While Slade was at work, I decided to go for a walk through the park. With the events of the last few months, the continual skirmishes between members of our rival clans, and the resulting stress of it all, having a few minutes of solace in the park had become my only getaway. As I walked along and watched the children play in the snow, I felt the weight of his eyes on me. The hairs on the back of my neck stood up, and a tingle ran down my spine. They were odd human sensations for a vampire to experience after the amount of blood I've drunk without a second thought, but they were there nonetheless.

The presence had a distinctly masculine quality, so I'd taken to referring to it as "him." Since he followed me religiously but didn't want to reveal himself, I decided to try waiting him out. An empty park bench caught my eye, so I took a seat at the end and waited, forcing him to wait with me or finally make himself known.

Hours I sat there in the cold with the wind whipping all around me. I never caught the slightest hint of his scent, but I could feel his energy near me. When he started feeling aggravated and restless, my determination renewed. The more impatient he became, the more likely he was to reveal himself and what he wanted with me.

After three hours, he finally sat on the opposite end of my park bench, but he kept his eyes averted from mine. His cat-and-mouse games had become tiresome, and I was past the point of allowing him to control the situation any longer. I shifted in my seat to face him directly and put this silliness behind us. If he was brazen enough to follow me in the day and night, he could be bold enough to face me and answer for his actions.

"Why are you following me?" I confronted him.

He had the audacity to appear affronted at my directness. "Excuse me? I'm not following you."

"You most definitely are following me. And you have been for quite some time now. You've waited here in the park for me to leave again. But your impatient nature got the best of you, so you sat beside me in a sad attempt to make me uncomfortable. Shall I continue?"

At least his discomfort was genuine. He swallowed hard, and the way his neck muscles worked revealed his inner plight. "You're more powerful than I realized."

"Who are you and what do you want?"

"My name is Rolland Cleary. I'm not following you to harm you. I was trying to determine the best way to approach you without causing another clan fight to erupt. I don't want your husband to find me and kill me."

"Do I really have to keep repeating myself?"

He finally turned to meet my gaze and gave me a half smile. "Who am I and what do I want, correct? I'm a vampire from another clan, from the old country, and we've heard about what Ramses has done. I'm here to offer my assistance with the whole situation."

"You're a vampire?" I asked, doubt shrouding my features and my tone.

He nodded, confirming I'd heard him correctly. But I knew better. However, to figure out what he was actually doing and who he really was, I decided to play along with his charade for a short time.

"Very well then, Vampire Rolland from the old country, tell me how you propose to assist with our current predicament. You have my full attention."

"I have certain gifts that could be useful to gain access to Ramses's clan and stop them from the inside. I could share my gift with your clan and also teach you how to use it."

Rolland Cleary is a handsome man in his midthirties. He has short black hair, dark brown eyes, and a naturally olive hue to his skin. He was very observant as we sat on the park bench. His eyes constantly scanned the area surrounding us. But what was he watching and waiting for?

"You want open access to our clan? To share your gift that can help us stop Ramses from whatever it is he's doing? All of this out of the goodness of your heart and without asking for anything in return?" My skepticism of his altruistic offer was impossible to hide.

"Stopping Ramses is all I need in return. To do that, your clan needs my help."

"Since you've been following me, you obviously know where we live. I suggest you come by and speak with my husband, our clan leader, rather than follow his wife for days on end. That could be misconstrued as aggression and result in your death."

Rolland's eyes narrowed slightly while he studied my face. His gaze traveled from my eyes to my lips and back up again. I had the distinct feeling the distrust went both ways. He wasn't certain he had me convinced of his usefulness, and I was in no way believing a word he said.

"I mean you no harm, I assure you. If your husband will see me and hear me out, I'll gladly speak to him."

"Wonderful. We'll expect you at seven tonight. In the meantime, I trust you've concluded your clandestine activities and will no longer be following my movements."

His cheeks tinged red with embarrassment from being so blatantly obvious. "I won't follow you anymore. You have my word."

I watched him walk away and smiled to myself. Olive-colored skin. No hint of blue vampiric eyes. Rose-colored cheeks after being embarrassed. There's not a chance in hell he is a vampire.

What he is, however, is a liar.

When I left the park, I went by Slade's office to tell him about my encounter with my watcher. He met me at the door when I walked in and wrapped his arms around me. With his nose buried in my hair, he murmured to me with his lips against my ear. "I'm so glad you came by to see me. Would it alarm you to know not more than three seconds ago, I was contemplating using my powers of persuasion to urge you to visit me?"

"I wouldn't be alarmed at all," I replied before kissing his cheek. "But you don't have to use your powers to persuade me to do anything. I'm all yours, whatever you want."

"My love, I will definitely remind you of that oath in all our years to come," he said with a sly smile. "Now, to what do I owe the pleasure of your company in the middle of the day?"

"The person who's been following me made himself known today. He says he needs to speak with you about how to stop Ramses. He claims to be a vampire from the old country, but I'm sure he's lying."

"Another man, a stranger, dared to follow and approach you? My wife? To say he needs to speak with me?" His chocolate brown eyes flashed to blue in an instant. "What is this fool's name?"

"Rolland Cleary."

"Should Mr. Cleary be brave enough to show his face in our home tonight, I'll be more than glad to have a long chat with him. Part of that chat will include what I think of him following my wife around day and night for the past few weeks."

"Have I told you lately how very sexy I think it is when your protective side takes over?"

"In that case, you and I will have fun *all night* after our guest leaves. *If* our guest leaves, I should say. That all depends on what he has to say. You're sure he's not a vampire?"

"I'm almost one hundred percent certain. If he is, he's unlike any I've sensed. I couldn't read his thoughts, but I could feel his power. He's strong, whatever he is. But there were too many discrepancies."

As I knew he would, Slade had me sit with him and recount every detail from the moment I first sensed Rolland through our entire conversation. When I'd finished, Slade was of the same mind-set—there's no way Rolland could be a vampire. But Slade also didn't know what he could be, so we'd have to be on our guard. He tried to persuade me to stay out of the meeting entirely, for my own safety, but I respectfully declined his request.

"If you think I won't be by your side to help protect my husband, you'd better think again." I folded my arms over my chest, and my glare dared him to object.

"It appears being a vampire agrees with my wife," he conceded with a single quirked eyebrow.

However, I didn't miss the flicker of pride in his expression. "Very well. But you're not to leave my side for any reason."

"You'll hear no argument from me on that point."

Chapter Thirteen

Slade Barnett, 1791

Alea sat by my side when our servants brought Rolland Cleary into our parlor. She was right about a couple of things—his power is strong, and he's not a vampire. But he can't fool me for one second. I saw straight through his ruse the moment he walked in the room, and he knew it. His hesitation was slight since he didn't want to give his true form away, but he approached the settee cautiously. As if he could get away if I didn't allow it.

"Have a seat." I extended my hand toward the chair beside me but on the opposite side of the room from Alea.

"Thank you for agreeing to meet with me. It's taking a calculated risk, I understand, but I appreciate the gesture of good faith."

My gaze stayed locked on his when I nodded my reply. It's my general policy not to lie to my prey. I prefer they know what's about to happen to them as a common courtesy. The last thing they need to hear before dying is a bold-faced lie. But Rolland was different since he blatantly shadowed my wife, lied to her face, and walked into my home with his ridiculous plan to deceive me.

"Mr. Cleary, you have something you'd like to discuss with my husband, I believe." Alea moved the conversation straight to the point. No pleasantries or small talk to become acquainted. I love my wife more than my own life, but my admiration for her is a close second.

"No need for formality. Please call me Rolland. I appreciate the hospitality you've shown me by inviting me into your home. Allow me to get straight to the point. I know what Ramses has been doing, and I want to help you stop him. My gifts are unique, and I've successfully transferred them to the members of my clan. I'm willing to do the same for you and your clan so you can get inside his and stop them before they reveal all of us."

"That's an interesting proposition, Rolland. You have my curiosity piqued. My wife mentioned you're from the old country. Tell me, how did you hear about Ramses and his current activities?"

"Word spread quickly when he returned to

London for Alea's friend, Sean. He wasn't discreet with his actions, and a number of well-aged vampires took special offense. They've cleaned up his mess in the area, but they will kill him if he returns."

"What do you know of his current activities?"

"My apologies, but can I trouble you for a drink? My throat is quite parched."

Rolland was trying to delay answering my direct question. But he had greatly underestimated me. If he wanted to play this game, I would be the one to teach him the rules.

"Where are my manners? Please accept my apologies." I summoned my servant and requested drinks for the three of us. When he returned with wineglasses of fresh, warm blood, unease passed over Rolland's face before he quickly hid his thoughts again.

Alea and I raised our glasses and drained them before the blood turned cold. Rolland raised his slowly and forced two sips down before he decided it was better to talk than to drink.

"You're aware Castel is here in New York, I presume?"

"I am."

"At Castel's command, Ramses closed up shop at his house nearby. But he has two other establishments that are even larger and more likely to reveal us. His clan is taking underage humans by the droves, and people are searching for them everywhere. It's attracted the attention of vampire hunters who know how to watch for the signs, but it's only a matter of time before it spills over to the general population."

Rolland wasn't wrong, which is why I decided to allow him to live. For the time being, at least. His information was helpful, though he was anything but trustworthy. Fortunately, I'd been able to decipher his subtle signs and distinguish his lies from the truth. I'll allow that to stand as long as I can tell the difference. But the first time I catch him in a lie I didn't detect ahead of time, I'll snap his neck.

"Vampire hunters are here, too?" Alea asked.

"Yes, they're here. That's another reason why time is of the essence, and why I'm here to help."

"Your solution is to share your gifts with us. What are your gifts, exactly?"

"I'm not comfortable sharing the specifics until I have an ironclad guarantee you and your clan agree. You have to understand, my gifts are powerful and not something I freely speak about."

He was evading giving us the true answer. His gifts were powerful, but there was more to them than he cared to reveal for a reason. Either they were something every other vampire would want and would kill to have...or they were something no other vampire would willingly accept if they knew the truth of the matter.

The obvious question was which category he fell into.

"I wasn't aware there was another vampire clan in the area. We normally sense when there are others nearby. We hold a meeting in a neutral location to set our clan boundaries. Then we respect the lines drawn in the proverbial sand. Strange you've known all about us, but the established vampire protocol hasn't been followed."

"Protocol in the new world has been slightly different from when we were first introduced to the life of a vampire. There are rogue vampires who refuse to be part of a clan. There are small clans scattered deep in the forests that kill other clans on sight. They don't respect lines or boundaries, and it takes quite a bit of time to scout other vampires to determine which philosophy they follow. That's why I followed your wife when I first sensed her presence. I didn't know what to expect, and I had to be sure."

"Interesting. I'm sure you'll understand when I say this is something I'll have to give considerable thought to before making a final decision. Accepting gifts without knowing what they are is not my usual style. However, vampire hunters, rogue vampires, and my brother's antics all lend concerning aspects to the overall problem before us. My council and I will discuss your proposal at length and apprise you of our decision."

"When shall I return for your answer?"

"We will come to you. Your invitation to our home is revoked until further notice. No offense intended, but in light of the news you've shared, I have to be diligent with the safety of my household. Oh and, Rolland? If you ever follow my wife again, the last thing you'll see is the light reflecting off my silver blade before it cuts your fucking head off. Are we clear?"

"Crystal clear."

Alea and I escorted him out of our house and retired to our bedroom to talk privately about what he'd said. Not that there was a chance in hell I'd accept his "gifts" without knowing what they were first, but my wife often brings incredible insight to perplexing issues.

"What are your thoughts?" I asked her. We lay in the bed, facing each other like mortals for the intimacy it evoked.

"I believe what he said about Ramses. There was no deceit in him when he described what Ramses's underground activities entail. But..." She paused to gather her thoughts. "He's hiding something about his gifts, and I haven't been able to pinpoint it. I can't read his thoughts and that alone is concerning, but I feel it strongly. I don't know what he is, but he's not a vampire. You already know this, but it would be a huge mistake to accept what he's offering."

"You're right, my love. He's not a vampire, not

a full vampire anyway. He's a vampire mixed with something else. The powers he's offering could be an incredible opportunity, or a grievous mistake. The way he insisted on sharing with the clan multiple times raises a dire warning in my mind. His offer is most likely an all-or-nothing proposal. We have to find out the full truth of everything before we send our regrets. Otherwise, we may lose them without knowing what threat they pose."

"Just tell me what to do. I'll be honored to help you figure it out."

"My love, I'll gladly tell you what to do. Starting right now. Prepare to scream my name until you rattle the windows."

I rolled her onto her back, covered her body with mine, and spent the night with my cock buried as deep in her pussy as I could fit. That's one thing I will never get my fill of. The sensations she gives me are overpowering at times, and my fangs automatically slide out to feast on her blood. Every drop only makes me crave her more.

Ramses Barnett, 1791

Castel's reappearance after decades of being away from us is suspect at best. I thought about it nonstop for weeks. Then I decided to do something about it rather than wallow in my uncertainty and madness for a moment longer.

He has many contacts all over the world, so I sought them out, looking for answers, searching for clues, piecing everything together to discover what he was hiding. I've replayed our entire conversation in my head at least a million times. My surprise at finding Slade in my house threw me off at first. Being pulverized by him when I was unable to use my powers to fight against his strength at all was the second distraction. Then Castel's appearance and disappearance were the icing on the cake.

Finding out Alea had been turned at the last possible second and how my yearning for her was even worse than before was the final straw. My ability to process everything was temporarily inhibited. But now I'm clearheaded, as clear as a bright, sunny day once the heavy fog has been burned away. The information I've collected from various clans and villages paints an interesting picture

In order to have a chance against him, I had to understand how he'd gained such incredible power and why his eyes turned red instead of the usual blue. The first point I learned was red-eyed vampires are extremely rare. Throughout the history of vampires' existence, less than a dozen red-eyes have ever been seen. Those who have had firsthand experience with them all recount the same basic information. For those few vampires who are chosen, the change first occurred when their loved one was in danger.

During my questioning of them, my contacts

frequently stressed these special ones are the strongest and fastest of all vampires. An added benefit to being at the top of the food chain is the ability to command lesser vampires. Changelings who haven't developed their own powers recognize them as their master—for all time, even after their powers emerge. They will leave the clan they were born into for their new master.

In addition to strength and speed, they can develop new powers as they're needed if they're under extreme duress. The new gifts may wane or revert back completely once they return to their normal state. This special skill makes killing them damn near impossible. The general speculation is they are also immune to silver's effects.

But the most fascinating fact I found was how the red eyes manifest in the first place. Part of the gift is transferred from the vampire who created him. The gift is completed when that vampire bonds with a family member of a very specific bloodline— the lineage of the Veiled Kings heritage.

Alea is the key to Slade's newfound power.

Assuming the facts that I've gathered are correct, I've come to the following conclusions. Slade has the power of the rare red-eyed vampire, and he has an incredibly strong bond with Alea, who is a direct descendant of the Veiled Kings' bloodline. Because of their bond, Slade's transformation is now complete, and the rare gift is now his.

Since Castel created Slade, Castel possessed the same power first and passed it on to Slade. But Castel also created me. Therefore, that must mean at least half of the same power resides in me at this moment. I only need the key to complete the transformation. My belief is Castel has already figured out this much and is working on a plan to take Alea for himself in order to unlock the power inside him and reach his full potential.

I have to find a way to entice Alea away from Slade before Castel does.

There's obviously no way I can court her while Slade is alive, or while Alea isn't under some sort of mind control—since she obviously holds ill will toward me for feeding on her. On the bright side, my actions did instigate her birth into her new life. Taking Slade's lifeblood will give me his powers. Theoretically, it is possible that I could keep her under my control. I could persuade her to fall in love with me instead of him.

Every step of this plan requires extreme caution and extraordinary coordination. Castel can't find out about my plan. Slade can't know I'm coming for him. Alea must be caught completely off guard. Even if those three points align, there's no guarantee my plan to persuade her will work. If Castel makes his move first, my entire plan is fucked up the ass, and there'll be no way to reverse the damage, unless someone kills him.

If another vampire discovers I killed my brother, my life will be over. I've narrowly escaped that judgment already. But the power calls to me. Alea beckons me. If not but for chance, Alea would be mine. Had I not been off setting up my secret locations and building my own clan numbers, she would've been mine. She should've been mine. I saw her first, I met her first, and I courted her first. As the eldest, the first choice should have been mine. Alea should be mine right now. The rest of the vampire world has to understand that. They will...eventually.

With this plan in mind, I began making my preparations. The brothel I run was my first stop. Castel has a healthy appetite for fucking and blood, guaranteeing he'll make his way there eventually. Setting a trap for him won't be easy, but I have an idea. If I don't tell the others my plans, the details won't be there when Castel reads their minds.

"Patrick, has a very old and powerful vampire been here while I was away?"

"No, not that I've been told."

"Good. Other business in the city must have kept him busy. When he arrives, you'll know him. His name is Castel. He was changed in his early fifties. His hair is black with dashes of gray throughout. He's a tad bit shorter than me, but he's fit and strong. He follows the old rules and style to the letter, including his clothes.

"He will expect this specific red Bordeaux. Do not allow anyone else to drink it. His tastes are very particular, and we need to keep him happy. Make sure the girls bathe every day, also. Multiple times, if necessary."

"Understood. I will see to it personally."

"Inform me at once when he arrives. No matter where I am or what I'm doing. This comes first."

After setting the stage at the brothel, my focus shifted to Slade. Trapping my brother would be more difficult. He'd smell my clan coming before they ever got close enough to speak to him. His dark gift would emerge if he had the slightest inclination Alea was in danger. Getting to him would require shrewd thought, meticulous planning, and flawless execution.

Fortunately, I'm an evil genius with a knack for accomplishing the impossible and a strong refusal to give up until I've succeeded. A week after leaving the special bottle of wine at the brothel for Castel, he showed up and drank the whole bottle. The strong sedative that would've killed a mortal man only lasted long enough to move him to an impenetrable room in the basement. He would be well cared for by my servants, but for obvious reasons, I had to stay far away from him.

Two weeks later, my entire plan for Slade and Alea was mapped out to the very last detail. Every man and woman in my clan was apprised of their specific role, and not one of them knew the entire plan. They were divided into several different teams and sent to specific locations to await my signal. When the conditions were perfect, I sent out the command and my army descended on Alea as she strode through the park. Alone. Within seconds, they'd grabbed her and were well on their way to my secret hideaway in the mountains upstate.

I sent one lady to their home, knowing Slade wouldn't be there, to leave a letter from Alea asking him to meet her in the park for a romantic stroll. Small teams were placed along the routes from his office to his home, and from his house to the location in the park. In the event he strayed off course, I wanted to know immediately. If he sensed any of my clan members, I would immediately send that team away to keep the rest of the mission on task. We had eyes on Slade at all times, watching his every step and every mood along the way.

We watched his every move, calculated his every expression, waited for him to arrive at the designated rendezvous point.

And that is exactly where it all went wrong.

The problem was we were so fixated on watching Slade, we didn't realize we were the ones being watched. We had no idea about the chain reaction of events our actions had set off. We had no forewarning of the full-scale war we'd started or how brutal it would be.

A war that, out of my foolishness and arrogance, *I'd* started.

Chapter Fourteen

Slade Barnett, 1791

"Slade, something is going to happen soon. I've had a vision." The warning in Thomas's tone was unmistakable.

"Alea?" I almost didn't want to ask, but if it was something I could change, I had to try.

"Yes, Alea. And you. And Castel. Ramses is at it again. His madness is reaching new levels. He's identified the source of your red-eyed power, and he wants it for himself."

"What's his plan?"

"He's going to sedate Castel and lock him in a silver-lined cell. He'll have his clan grab Alea while she's out on one of her walks in the park. Then they'll use her to lure you to the same place so

Ramses can kill you himself. He wants your blood so he can take your powers.

"*He thinks Castel is already planning to do something similar to unlock his own inner power. Ramses's obsession with this power is driving him to make rash decisions that will get him killed.*"

"*As if these random clan attacks he's orchestrated haven't been bad enough. He'll create an all-out war in the streets with no regard for the collateral damage it'll cause. We need to make our preparations to counteract this insane plan of his now. When he makes his move, our countermove must put a stop to all this madness.*"

That conversation with Thomas occurred not twenty-four hours before Ramses made his move on Alea. I'd made arrangements with Castel to pay a visit to my home and meet my wife. I wanted to introduce her to the man who gave me this life. I wanted him to meet my immortal love.

On my way home from my office, I sensed all the eyes watching me. I caught the scent of Ramses's clan on the wind. I heard the thoughts of those young ones who were inexperienced and too stupid to be on their own when they dared to get too close to me. I knew it was the beginning of Thomas's vision.

When I entered my house and found the fake note from Alea, I knew Thomas had already put our counter-strike into play. Moments after I walked in,

Thomas came in behind me with Castel in tow.

"Hello, my boy. It seems your brother has a bone to pick with you and me." Castel smiled cheekily at me.

"It would seem so. What'd you do to him?" I retorted with my own snarky smile.

"Thomas filled me in on the plan when he sprang me from that prison cell. You know I can't kill Ramses, but I'll gladly help you stop him. Shall we?" Castel gestured toward the door.

The monster inside was clawing at me to let him out. He wanted to end this once and for all by ending Ramses. I held him at bay, locked in his own prison cell inside my head. It took mere seconds for us to reach the front line of the clan war in progress, but the sight of the carnage was worse than I could've imagined.

Vampires who should've been taught to stand for each other, instead tore each other apart. Silver blades slid through the air with lightning speed, held by men who should be brothers and women who should be sisters. The orders shouted telepathically in their heads repeated "Kill them all" over and over again, almost like a chant to brainwash them. My clan was forced to kill their own kind or be killed themselves.

They'd been created for the purpose of protection and overthrowing rival clans. But that was exactly the problem—other clans should never have been viewed as competition. A clan is a family, and other clans have always been considered to be extended families. There have always been cases of wayward vampires, the ones who go off on their own and cause too much trouble for the rest to cover. They've always been dealt with individually.

But what Ramses has created is an abomination, only in the size of an entire clan. He's taught and trained them in his irrational and psychotic ways. As long as they're under his dominion, they'll labor under the same folly and recklessness Ramses does.

"Slade, call your clan off. I'll have Ramses do the same," Castel commanded before he disappeared.

I called to my members and ordered them to a neutral location. The shorter daylight hours of the winter were a blessing in disguise, thankfully ensuring the darkened park was empty of humans. The decapitated heads of vampires from my clan and Ramses's clan littered the snow-covered ground. Crimson stains from their blood tainted the white snow, turning the once serene park into a combat zone. Vampires from both houses died unnecessarily because envy and obsession ruled my brother's actions instead of rational thoughts.

Castel approached me with my brother following closely behind him. He stopped short of where I stood, knowing full well he didn't want to engage in a direct fight with me.

"Ramses, what have you done?" Castel asked as

he moved through the battlefield remnants, taking in the full weight of the night's massacre.

"I-I..." He stuttered, but couldn't form a reply.

Ramses's eyes met mine, and I watched as shame and regret filled them. My brother loved me—in his own twisted way. But I think he envied me more than he loved me, and he was obsessed with my wife. Then he plotted to murder me so he could take her for himself. As much as I've tried to overlook or correct his erratic behavior over the last century, I can't deny my efforts appear to have been in vain.

"Ramses, you locked me in a cell. You planned to ambush and murder your brother. You had your men take his wife. What do you have to say for yourself?" Castel leveled his gaze on Ramses and waited for him to explain himself.

Ramses wavered between rage and regret. His eyes darted back and forth between Castel's and mine. Then his expression changed to pure hatred and I knew what would come next, but he sprinted away before I could grab him. His clan left on his heels and disappeared into the night, carrying the bodies of their dead.

"Don't worry. I know where he went," Castel assured me. "I'll keep an eye on him and try to help him as best I can. You have to prepare yourself for the possibility that he'll completely turn from me and I'll lose my hold on him."

"I know. It's a good thing we've never told him he had that option before. He would've been much worse now if he'd known in the earlier years."

"I also can't guarantee another vampire won't kill him for what he's done."

"Put the word out for everyone to stay out of my fight. It's my wife and my clan he's after. That makes it my right to handle in my own way. If anyone takes that from me, I'll have his head."

"Slade, you can't save your brother, regardless of how hard you try. That's not what you want to hear, but it's the truth. We've both known it for many years now."

Despite all Ramses has done over the years, I never really gave up on him changing from his destructive path. I've always wanted to believe the best of my older brother. But a bigger part of me knew he was right, and I also knew Castel couldn't watch him all the time. Castel would soon travel back to his home and his clan. He came to help us, but I couldn't and wouldn't expect him to do more than he already had.

Dealing with Ramses fell on my shoulders and mine alone. All that stays my blade is I know most of his actions stem from his addled brain. That's something he can't help. But how far do I let that go in the name of family? At what point do I put the overall good first, rather than my loyalty to family and blood?

My sole comforting thought as I walked home was knowing my wife was waiting for me there. The only thing I want to do for the rest of the night is bury myself balls deep inside her and not quit until the sun rises in the west, blocking the rest of the world and its problems from our minds for all of eternity. But first, we would entertain our guest and put the unpleasantness of the night behind us for a short time. The time when I'm forced to make a final decision will come soon enough.

Alea Barnett, March 1791

Ramses has been in hiding since the night in the park that will forever go down in infamy. I can't say I'm sorry he's not near us, but the concern is etched in my dear husband's face just the same. Especially in light of what happened to me that night in the park—an event we haven't shared with anyone else out of concern of sparking yet another clan war.

Slade arrived home from the confrontation between the two clans first, and I've never been so happy and relieved to see him as I was that night. When he walked through the door, like a normal, human husband would do after a long day at work, I was waiting not so patiently on the other side. I rushed into his embrace, and he picked me up in his strong arms, not uttering a single word while he pressed my chest into his. I wrapped my legs around his waist and my arms around his neck and clung to him for dear life.

I knew Castel would be along soon, and there was something I needed to share with Slade before our guest arrived. Though I hated to break the intrinsic connection we'd established, time wasn't on my side.

"Slade, I need to tell you what happened to me in the park tonight, before Castel arrives." Keeping my voice low and controlled was an intentional move. I know my husband and his protectiveness of me all too well. My hope was he'd remain calm as long as I was calm when sharing how the events unfolded.

His hand crawled up my scalp, weaving my hair between his fingers as he moved. With a light, sensual tension, his fingers curled into a loose fist, and he pulled my head back so we were face-to-face. "Did one of them hurt you?"

His voice was calm, but the fire in his eyes was lit and burned brightly. I held his face in my hands and kissed his full lips. "No, no one hurt me. But I love how you're ready to take on the world single-handedly for me in an instant. It seems you've passed the power of the red eyes on to me."

"You're serious?"

"Deadly."

At first, he was thrilled we shared such a rare gift.

There was never any doubt, but this oddity further demonstrated we were destined to be together. Then concern and hesitation stole the joy of the moment when he had to face the ramifications this twist held. Ramses was already obsessed with me and with unlocking the inner power, but knowing I also possessed it would ensure he'd try again.

"What happened?"

"Two of his men grabbed me and tried to fly away with me. It happened so fast, I didn't even realize where the extra power came from at first. But in the black sky, the glow from my eyes was reflected on their faces."

"If his clan members saw it, then he already knows. It's not safe for you here."

"No, they couldn't have told him. I killed them both and flew back home."

"He's linked to them telepathically. You're sure they didn't convey it to him before they died?"

"I'm positive. I could hear their thoughts, and I could block their connection to him."

"You never cease to amaze me, Alea. Just when I think you couldn't impress me more, you find a way to prove me wrong."

"When you explained where it came from, I never expected I'd also have it. But it does make sense. Castel passed it to you from his blood, and you passed it to me from your blood."

"And with that gift residing in you, my dear,

your abilities will be more powerful than anyone could possibly imagine," Castel said, appearing beside us out of thin air.

"Castel, perfect timing, my friend." Slade released me to stand beside him while he made introductions between Castel and me.

Castel pulled me into a friendly embrace after kissing my cheeks. "We are family now, Alea. I will love you like my own daughter, and I hope in time you will come to love me as a second father. Slade and Ramses are very dear to me, though I don't condone Ramses's actions in the slightest."

His thick Italian accent was soothing. His sincerity made me feel loved and a welcome addition to a large family, the one thing my parents were never able to provide. The love he has for the two men he considers to be his sons is genuine, as is the pain he felt when Ramses betrayed him.

"Thank you, Castel. Your kindness means a great deal to me. As does your love for Slade. What Ramses has done isn't your fault or your responsibility. It's admirable how you still try to help and guide him, but he's a grown man and he makes his own decisions."

"I'm grateful my son has found his soulmate— and even more thrilled that soulmate is you, Alea. You both must come stay with me in my village soon. I believe you will love it there."

We spent the rest of the evening talking with

Castel, hours of sharing stories about family, our homes, and what we have to look forward to in the future. He spoke of Slade and Ramses—how they became his sons and how I could look forward to embracing younger vampires as my children one day. To clarify, he meant my children-to-be would be younger in the time they'd been vampires, not in human years. Regardless, the concept gave me even more hope for our future.

Hours later, Castel announced he was returning to the countryside in Italy rather than staying in the new world with us any longer. "You'll find Ramses hidden at this location." He pointed to a spot on the map that was in the mountains in the northern area of New York state. "He's built an enormous house deep in the forest. So deep, it won't be found by humans for many years to come. However, I don't believe he's given up on his illicit plans. If he continues on his current path, he'll soon consort with shifters. That cannot be allowed, Slade."

"Shifters?" I asked and cut my questioning eyes to Slade.

"Shapeshifters, love. Intermingling of species is forbidden," he explained.

I realized there is so much I don't know about this magical world. So many powers to discover and develop. There are so many answers to find, yet I don't even know what the correct questions are to ask. When I looked up at Castel, I knew he'd read my thoughts from his perceptive smile. He placed his hand on my shoulder as a sign of support.

"Slade and Alea, you both have to stop fighting the *maestro rosso* inside you to let it live and breathe. The more you use it, the stronger it'll become. You have no reason to fear it, my children. Embrace it, nurture it, and allow it to teach you powers you've never even dreamed of. I promise, you won't regret it." He smiled warmly and knowingly when he finished speaking. Then his eyes glowed bright red right before he disappeared as quickly as he'd first appeared.

I turned to Slade and linked my fingers with his. "He is wonderful, Slade. It would be amazing to take him up on his offer to visit his village in Italy."

"For you, anything."

"About what he said just before he disappeared. I have an idea that may make it easier on us both to release control and free the *maestro rosso* in both of us." I couldn't help but smile as the idea formed in my mind.

"Do go on." The sexy timbre of his voice and the seductive shimmer in his gaze said he knew what I was about to suggest.

"The first one to suppress the red glow becomes the other's sex slave for the next month."

"I'm thrilled with the initiative you're taking, but I don't see a loser in this wager." His eyes instantly changed to red, his voice became deeper, and I felt his hands groping my body, but he didn't move a finger. "All of this already belongs to me."

Not to be outdone, I matched his fervor with my own move. With my mind and body relaxed, I let go of the control I thought I had and turned it over to the red master inside. When Slade felt the warmth of my mouth wrap around the head of his cock, his head dropped back, his eyes closed, and his moans urged me to continue.

In a flash, I was in his arms, and we instantly transported to the privacy of our bedroom. He murmured in my ear, his voice gravelly and thick with desire. "Now I want to feel you suck me off for real this time."

"My pleasure, *il mio maestro rosso. Il mio amore immortale.*"

My red master. My immortal love.

"You're already learning to speak Italian. I have to say, hearing that from your mouth is so damn sexy. Although, it's still not nearly as sexy as the other talents your mouth has."

With a lascivious smile, I dropped to my knees in front of him, relieved him of his trousers, then completely relieved him. He was more than ready for me as I licked the tip of his cock, spreading the bead of moisture around the rim. My mouth watered from just thinking about what more was to come. Without warning, I took as much of his length as I could in me until the tip of his cock hit the back of my throat. His resulting moan and the way he gripped my hair spurred my enthusiasm. I increased my speed and my grasp, his hips met my surges in a perfect rhythm until I felt the warmth of his release in my mouth ebb.

"You are so fucking perfect." With swift moves, he whisked me up from the floor and pushed my back against the wall. "Now it's my turn. Or rather, your turn." His sexy smirk was in place while he removed my clothes and licked his way down my body. He started with my breasts, slid his tongue down my stomach, and stopped at my already swollen clit. "Hold on tight, baby. I'm hungry enough to eat all night."

Chapter Fifteen

Slade Barnett, 1791

I think the only thing more concerning than Ramses starting a clan war is Ramses being completely silent. Since the night he sprinted away from Castel and me, he has remained secluded in his mountain hideaway. We've both kept tabs on him and his activities. Castel reappears when he's able to leave his home in Sardinia, though he doesn't tell Ramses he's there. I vaporize in and out in much the same manner, but for very different reasons.

I'm not as concerned with Ramses's well-being as Castel is. I still want him dead. When I check on him, it's because I'm focused on his actions. From what I've seen, not much has changed, except he has kept his business private rather than flaunting his indiscretions with pride. I would say my hope is he learned a lesson after all the trouble he caused, but then he'll simply disappoint me again. Some things never change. Some people refuse to change.

There have been so many times I've stood directly beside him, my silver blade firmly held in my grasp. The visions of all his infractions against me clear in my mind. The deep need for retribution damn near consuming me. Yet I've shown considerable restraint, all in the name of keeping the peace between us for Castel's sake. Out of deference and love for the man who became our father when we lost our parents, I've allowed Ramses to live against every fiber in my body telling me otherwise.

While I'd prefer to monitor him from afar, neither Castel nor I can use our powers to see or hear what he's doing. We've concluded Ramses has vampires in his immediate circle who have developed a talent for hiding his secrets from us. His own personal bodyguards, so to speak, who have no idea how ineffective they'd be should I decide to terminate their employment. It's these thoughts that stoked the fire of my wrath. When I was close to giving in to my rage, I came home to my wife, and just one look at her calmed the erupting volcano inside me.

"Why are you staring at me?" she asked.

"The real question is how can I not stare you?"

"Would you like to tell me what's bothering you?"

"You know me inside and out," I remarked. "But no, I don't want to talk about it. You are my escape from everything that bothers me."

Her responding nod confirmed she understood what I meant. The mood instantly lightened as she wrapped her arms around my neck and kissed me.

"You need to feed, my love," she urged. "I'd say you've missed a meal or two from the pallor of your skin. Shall we go out to eat tonight?"

"You must have read my mind," I quipped. "Lady's choice tonight."

We left the house on the prowl for our next meal with my wife in the lead. The opera had just concluded, and many of the old English money-holders emerged. Alea turned to me and smiled deviously. I burst out laughing at the irony she conveyed wordlessly.

"Blue bloods? Perfect choice, my love." I kissed her on the cheek. "Enjoy your meal."

We each chose our prey and employed our hunting tactics. My victim was a lady of noble descent. I knew this mainly because she made it a point to tell everyone within earshot. Her pride and pompous attitude made her even more repulsive to me. The scent of her blood increased my hunger—and my ferocity.

"Darling, walk me home. It's not appropriate

for a true Lady to wander about without being accompanied by a gentleman," she insisted.

The young man she spoke to was visibly hesitant to oblige her. She was insistent and obnoxious. He searched for a polite way to excuse himself and get out of his predicament.

"I do wish I could be of assistance to you, my dear. But I have already promised another I'd escort her home."

With that, he joined another group of people and was blatant in his actions to be seen with a young woman on his arm. The group disappeared around the corner of the block, leaving Miss Lady Blue Blood all alone. Most of the opera-goers dissipated into carriages or walked the few blocks to their brownstones.

"What is a beautiful lady like yourself doing walking alone?" I asked pointedly, pouring salt into her open wound under the guise of a veiled compliment. "That should be considered a crime."

"I'm afraid my male companion had an urgent matter arise. I insisted he leave the opera early to attend to his sick mother."

"That's very gracious of you. May I escort you home in his stead?" I extended the crook of my arm for her, and she readily accepted.

"You're quite the gentleman. That's a quality which is, unfortunately, becoming harder to find in men of late."

Two blocks later, she was still talking about the decline in manners and decorum at court, how her family was close to the royal family, and how any man would be more than fortunate to marry her. On the quiet, dark sidewalk, I decided I'd heard enough, and she'd run out of time. While she was so self-absorbed with her high-level connections, I extended my fangs and clamped down on her neck. My hand covered her mouth to muffle her scream.

Her cry was short-lived, as was she since I was hungrier than I'd realized. I drained her blood in record time and disposed of her body far away from the city and the people. When I returned, a drunk man, stumbling as he walked and holding on to the buildings to keep him upright, became my next victim. My dessert, as it turned out. The alcohol sweetened his blood just enough to satisfy my appetite.

On my way back to find Alea, I sensed a presence I hadn't felt in many years. Living as and mingling with humans as long as I have, I've done my best to blend in and not call attention to what I really am. But this presence is actively looking for me. Searching for me since he first suspected me nearly a decade ago.

On one of my travels, I visited Spain, looking for new hunting grounds and new blood to add to my palate. I was in no hurry to feed when I arrived in the country. The culture was vastly different from what I'd grown accustomed to in London. Strolling through the streets of Madrid on summer's eve, a group of girls approached me from the opposite direction. They were absolutely stunning—every one of them. They were all close in age, but only a year or two separated each of them in a stair-step manner.

Sisters. From oldest to youngest, the five young ladies' ages spanned from twenty-two to sixteen years old. The younger ones giggled when they looked at me, but the oldest was clearly as taken with me as I was with her.

"Hello, lovely young ladies." I tipped my hat and gave them my best smile.

"Hello, sir," the oldest, Daniela, replied. "You flatter us."

"You deserve to be flattered." I lifted her hand and pressed my lips against the back of her palm. The scent of her blood was pleasant and calming. Her skin smelled of lavender, a floral and sweet aromatic fragrance I can still smell today.

Daniela and I became fast friends while I was on holiday in Madrid. She introduced me to her father, a local farmer from the outskirts of the city, and I instantly liked him. He was a tall, robust man who'd never met a stranger in his life. He was welcoming and inviting to anyone who entered his home.

For the most part, I'd eliminated my human reactions and feelings, but her father's open acceptance touched a small part of me where human fondness had found a place to hide. Before I left the area, I set the family up with a farming contract to supply a produce seller in Madrid for many years to come. The payments the farmer would receive for his farm goods would ensure his family's comfort and security.

I returned to the area a few years later and visited the farm to check on the man and his family. They were all gone, the farm had become a mess of overgrowth and neglect, and the home bore numerous religious symbols with crucifixes hanging everywhere. In that moment, I knew, but I didn't want to face the truth.

I rushed to the neighbors on both sides of the farm and began asking questions about the family. What had happened to them? Where had they gone? Why was the farm abandoned? Superstition ruled the small farming community, forcing me to go into Madrid to find anyone who could tell me what had happened. The produce seller remembered me and agreed to share the family's fate when no one else would.

From what I was able to piece together of his story, I was positive a rogue vampire had moved through the area and possibly picked up my scent at the farm. When the neighbors went to check on the family after they hadn't seen them for several days, they found the parents and all five daughters mutilated.

Convinced their deaths could've only been caused by demons, the outlying townspeople covered the desecrated home in crucifixes to ward them off. The grocer finished his story and wiped the tears from his eyes. I returned to the farm to look at it with new eyes and a renewed purpose.

I walked through the small farmhouse with its meager possessions, remembering the abundance of love that flowed to all who entered into these four walls. All but one, anyway.

That's when I smelled his scent. That's when I knew.

"What are you looking for, sir?" His smug tone taunted me, as he intended.

"The monster who killed this family."

"You're looking in the wrong place, then. Come. I'll show you what he looks like."

I followed the man into the family room, waiting for him to reveal his game. He moved to a large piece of furniture draped with a sheet.

"He's in here." The stranger smirked. He jerked the sheet off, revealing an armoire with a full panel mirror on the front.

His mouth dropped open, and his eyes flew wide open as his gaze darted back and forth between the mirror and me.

"But...but..." he stuttered, dumbfounded.

"Is this your idea of a joke?" My nostrils flared,

and my voice dropped by a couple of octaves.

"You have a reflection."

"Of course, I do. What kind of lunatic are you? I'm here to find out what happened to my friend and his family, but you waste my time with this absurd behavior. Why are you here anyway?"

"I thought... I was sure you were a..."

"A what?" I roared.

"I hunt and kill vampires. I was sure you were a vampire and had turned this family." His face was horror-stricken when he turned to look at his own reflection.

"You killed this family because you thought they were vampires?"

Tears slipped from his eyes, and he continued to stare at the monster in the mirror. The one he considered to be the monster. "Yes." His reply came out as a hoarse whisper, haunted and ashamed.

"You bastard!" I changed before his eyes and lunged for him. His reaction time was delayed, but he was well equipped for hunting vampires.

As my hand closed around his throat, he slashed my arm with a silver blade. My automatic reaction was to release him and withdraw my arm from the searing pain. In retrospect, I regret not ignoring the pain and finishing what I'd started.

In my momentary lapse of judgment, the vampire hunter scrambled away. I rushed out to catch him and kill him, but I found him having an animated conversation with passing neighbors. Rather than kill all of them, I left the area out of respect for the memory of my friends. But I committed his scent to memory.

When I caught that same scent after feeding, I realized at least one of the warnings Rolland had issued on his visit was true. Vampire hunters are here, adding yet another level of danger to an already volatile situation. After replaying his visit and the conversation, I have to question if he actually wanted to warn me, or if he intended to bring the vampire hunters directly to me.

I think it may be time to have another talk with Rolland Cleary.

Chapter Sixteen

Alea Barnett, July 1791

I'm almost afraid to write the next sentence out of fear it'll jinx us. It's been months since we've seen or heard a single word about Ramses. Slade and I finally have had time to enjoy being married without the added stresses of clan skirmishes, Ramses's madness, or the possibility of having our true nature revealed to the world. For the last several months, we've solely focused on our life together and what we want out of it.

With Slade being the sole proprietor of his business, his workload doubled when he was forced to pick up the slack for his brother's customers. Not seeing my husband wasn't an option, so I joined him in the office and helped with the financial negotiations and collecting commissions. On the rare occasions a customer ventured into the office, it was easy to explain my presence there was simply to assist my husband for a short time. After all, it's not prim and proper for a lady of my stature to work outside the home. The general consensus in this era is I should be home, barefoot and pregnant, tending to the other children, and making my home comfortable for my husband when he finishes a hard day in the office.

My feisty side has proven to be harder and harder to keep in check lately. My *maestro rosso* wants to come out and play at the most inappropriate times. Humans aren't as likely to appreciate the glowing red eyes as much as other vampires do. However, when a man comes in and speaks to me in a condescending tone, it's all I can do to stop myself from ripping his throat out.

Slade is truly the best man for me. When I first shared my frustrations with him, he tried to hide his smile behind his hand. That lasted all of about two seconds before his booming laughter filled his office. Watching his gorgeous face light up was worth all the frustration the ignorant men cause me. I realized at that moment he hadn't had a good reason to laugh like that in far too long. With all the problems his brother had caused, Slade was the one who was left to pick up the scattered and tattered pieces after Ramses disappeared. Any excuse I can find to make him smile, laugh, smirk, or be as proud of me as I am of him is worth whatever it takes.

We worked side by side until everything was caught up and Slade could take an extended break. I wanted to take Castel up on his offer to visit his village and get Slade away for the alone time we'd missed out on. Sometimes convincing him to take time away from the office required unconventional methods. While he sat in his office chair, reviewing the business expansion plans, I crept up beside him and straddled his lap before he could stop me. His body's reaction to mine was immediate—and more than a little stimulating.

"Mrs. Barnett, is there something I can do for you?"

I nodded. "Yes, Mr. Barnett. I'm afraid you're the only one who can help me with this little problem I have."

"By all means, tell me what I can do to you." His hands began roaming, and his eyes no longer focused on my face but fell to my breasts. Right where his hands were headed.

"You meant to say 'for me,' correct?"

"Of course. What can I do for you, or to you, or with you? Same difference."

His hands slid under my blouse to cup my breasts, while mine slid down his chest, past his rippled stomach, to take hold of his cock and tell him what I wanted him to do to me. He loves when I give him explicit details. Of course, I secretly love telling him—mostly because of how much it affects him and all the benefits I get out of it in return. "I want you to let me fuck you right here in this chair. I can sit right here in your lap and take all of you inside me."

He pushed my panties to the side, freed his cock from his pants, and buried himself inside me to the hilt in one swift motion. The way he filled and stretched me left an immediate sensation of pain and pleasure combined in the most delicious way. His fingers gripped my hips as he lifted his, driving into me as I pushed downward onto him. Keeping my screams muffled was the hardest thing I've ever done. Part of the time, it was because my fangs were dug into his neck. The rest of the time, it was because he swallowed my screams with his orgasm-inducing kisses.

He stood, taking me with him, and sat me on his desk with my skirt pushed up around my waist. "These are in my way." He slid my panties off, slipped his hands behind my knees, and yanked me to the edge of the desk. "A couple of my clients warned me you'd be a distraction in the office. I didn't agree with them at first, but maybe I've changed my mind."

"Am I distracting you?" My tone was overly sweet and innocent, but my red eyes were a dead giveaway of my deception. I nonchalantly opened my legs wider, clearly playing with fire and asking to be burned.

His predatory smile was nothing short of a work of art, turning his already gorgeous face more godlike. When his gaze lowered to my opened legs, his chocolate bedroom eyes became smoldering embers of red-hot desire, boring a hole through me and heating me from the inside out. "I don't know. I forgot what I was saying. But you should hold on, because this desk is about to move."

With only a moment's warning, he thrust into me again, shoving the desk back with his force. My eyes closed of their own accord from the abruptness of his welcomed intrusion. My body knows its master is Slade and is more than willing to submit to whatever he wants. The room filled with the sensual sounds of our feverish lovemaking. The wood desk sliding back and forth across the wood floor. Slick skin slapping against skin. Guttural moans, grunts, sighs, and whimpers emanated from everywhere, echoing off the walls and returning to us as a rapturous symphony.

Slade looped his arms around my legs, shifted his angle, and drove into me with a renewed fierceness. With every strike, he hit the exact spot deep inside me that left me powerless to prevent my loud cry, followed by violent shudders that racked my body. It was by far the most exquisite experience he's given me to date. And that's saying quite a bit.

Once we'd regained our professional composure, he kissed me softly and palmed my cheek, rubbing his thumb lovingly over my face. "Was there something else you wanted to talk to me about? Or were your intentions solely to distract me, seduce me with your charms, and have your wicked way with me?"

"Do I need another reason to schedule a meeting with my husband?" I feigned insult.

One eyebrow crept slowly toward his hairline in a sexy, dominant challenge.

"Maybe there was one other thing I wanted to bring up."

"I'm waiting." He folded his thick, muscular arms over his chest. His intimidating stance didn't scare me. If anything, it only added to his overall appeal.

"I was hoping since we've caught up on everything around here, we could take Castel up on his offer to visit him in Italy. You and I could use a long holiday, just the two of us, to get away to paradise on earth."

"You know, you may be more than just a distraction. You may actually be a complete interruption to my business. How can I ever deny you anything you ask?"

"Is it wrong I hope never to find out the answer to that question?"

"Fly home and pack our bags. I'll finish up

here in a few hours, without your interference, and we'll leave tonight. Tomorrow, we'll be strolling the beach in utopia."

Slade Barnett, 1791

Alea's suggestion to go to Castel's for a private getaway for just the two of us couldn't have come at a better time. Ramses, Rolland, and the unnamed vampire hunter—they've consumed enough of my time and energy, on top of running my business. Too much focus has been taken away from my wife, and that's not acceptable.

Since the night I realized the hunter was in my city, I've roamed the streets and searched for him. Was he alone? Did he know I was here? Will he come after my Alea? These questions have haunted me and pushed me closer to obsession.

Closer to understanding Ramses.

The idea, the nightmare, of someone getting to my wife and taking her from me is enough to make me as crazy as Ramses. To make me do things I'd otherwise never even consider. Like hunting for a vampire hunter on my own. One who has already escaped from me once before. One I am close to locating and will have another talk with very soon.

My wife's plan to whisk me away to an Italian paradise was just what the doctor ordered. Sensing our need to be alone, Castel opened his home to us then made himself scarce. I never appreciated how magnificent his home was in my vampire youth. At first, my thoughts were consumed with the death of my parents. As time normally does, it dulled the ache left by their absence, and I focused on becoming the most powerful vampire possible.

But my return to this oasis was markedly different. Alea and I returned to a simpler time in our lives. We've taken strolls on the beach at sunset, drank fine wines on the lanai overlooking the water, interacted with the local villagers at the town market, and made love every night like newlyweds.

"This has been such a magical week, Slade. Thank you for closing the office and bringing me here."

"It has been all my pleasure, I assure you."

Alea lay naked on the bed, the breeze from the ocean blowing through the window. It carried her scent, filled the room with it, and completely covered me. I've pinpointed why her scent neither incites me to feed nor calms me to indifference. Why she both incites me to love and calms me to indifference toward anything and anyone else in the world.

She is my fate. My soul. *My very soul.*

I ran my hand over her naked body, lost in the perfection that is my wife. We'd drunk our fill earlier in the evening far away from our island paradise, so her skin was warm to the touch and soft to feel. I leaned over and drew her breast into my mouth.

Looking up into her eyes, I had a thought I wish I could make a reality. "For you, Alea, I'd close my business and stay here, feasting on your love."

"Don't tempt me, Slade. That's a very dangerous offer because I'd love nothing better than to do just that."

"If we could survive on our love alone, it would be perfect. Since the world revolves around currency rather than bartering, I'm afraid income is required."

"So we return to our home and our lives tomorrow and save this time in our memory. We'll return again soon—we'll make it a point to visit Castel and keep him an active member of our family."

"That's just one reason why I love you, Alea. You know exactly what I need before I even know myself."

What I did know was I didn't want to return to New York or our current lives or my current job. Because no matter how long I stayed away, I knew some sort of trouble would await my return. Something that would steal the joy I'd rediscovered with Alea in Sardinia.

For some reason, the trouble in my life has always started with Ramses.

Alea Barnett, May 1791

That feeling of being watched won't leave me. I

know all too well how to blend in with humans. And I know when I'm being followed. It's difficult to disappear into thin air on the streets of New York City with how crowded they are during the workday. But that's exactly what I've considered doing many times lately when the feeling of imminent threat hovers over me.

After several days in a row of the growing threat around me, I mentioned my concerns to Slade.

"Where are you when you feel it the strongest?"

"On the street just outside your office. From the time I turn the corner on the block until I reach your office. On my way home, I find different routes and fly as soon as I'm out of sight," I explained.

Slade stared at me for several heartbeats with an intensely concerned expression. "Maybe you should stay home for a while instead of coming here to my office during the day."

"So you want me to hide away because of this feeling?"

"It may be wise."

"What are you not telling me, Slade? What is it you know about this?"

He hesitated for only a moment before replying. "It's not anything I know outright yet. It's more of a familiar feeling."

Then he told me about what he'd encountered in Madrid several years ago. The family he'd befriended were slaughtered by a vampire hunter who thought they'd been changed. Then that man tried to kill Slade. Now Slade thinks that same man may be here and could be watching me.

"I refuse to be confined to my home under lock and key because someone may be here to kill us. We are lethal adversaries, my love. I say we take the fight to him. Draw him out into a trap to put an end to this before he has a chance to strike at us."

"I admit I have considered the same plan. My only hesitancy is if he should hurt you, my dear. It will not end well for him, me, or anyone else in this city if I lose you."

"And I feel no less passionately about you. That just means we work together and make sure we both walk away intact—but he doesn't."

I could tell he didn't like it from his furrowed brow to the heavy sighs that are wholly unnecessary for vampires. He didn't hesitate to use them when the context called for it. I suppose it's also a carryover response from working with human clients day in and day out. Either way, he's so cute when he does it.

He summoned Thomas, and we began planning the trap for our vampire hunter. Thomas has taken Ramses's place at the business and has been a great help to Slade.

"I haven't had any visions about a hunter, but I've had strong feelings of being watched on my way to the office. If it's the same guy, we need to take him out of the picture immediately. I'm all for making the first move."

"So what's the plan?" Slade asked.

"My thought is he must have a place on the same street as your office because that's where we feel his presence the strongest. We should go on a hunt there ourselves. One feeds, the other two watch for him, then grab him when he shows his face," I explained.

"It would have to be late at night. This area is still fairly crowded in the evening hours. We'd be taking a chance he'd be asleep as late as we'd be out there," Slade countered.

"Or maybe he sleeps during the day and goes out to hunt at night. Maybe that's why we always feel him in the same area but he never does anything to us," I replied.

"It's worth a try," Thomas said. "That theory makes sense."

"It does make sense, because I've searched for him at night in different areas around the city but haven't felt him. I haven't gone back to that area because of the crowds." Slade dropped his head in his hands and grunted loudly. "Fine. Let's do it late tonight and get it over with before I change my mind."

"Slade, you do realize it may take more than one night? We're guessing about his sleeping habits. And just because he sleeps there doesn't mean that's where he hunts. We'll possibly have to move around the city until we sense him," Thomas replied.

"I hate this idea more with every word you two say," Slade complained.

Every night for the following two weeks, we fed and waited for the hunter to emerge from the shadows. We moved our trap to different areas of the city, extended our hunting areas to the outer limits of the city. When I suggested we isolate the hunter during the day, when he's likely sleeping, Slade was adamant that would never happen.

But then, he's very busy with clients during the day.

Now that Thomas works with him, they've taken on additional clients, and business has been booming again. While they've been preoccupied with work, I've quietly followed my senses until I located the elusive vampire hunter. I watched him for a moment while he slept in the middle of the day. He looked so young and peaceful in sleep. Then suddenly he spoke and I prepared to vaporize away, but I realized he was talking in his sleep.

He was having a bad dream, fighting something or someone for his life. A vampire, I guessed.

Since I know where he is, I know where to wait and watch for him to leave. I'll soon find out where he's been hunting and where we could set our trap. And catch him. I thought about killing him myself in that tiny one-room apartment that was more the size of a broom closet. But he may not be alone in his quest.

But the main reason I left him alive was because of what he'd done to my husband. Slade deserved the opportunity to exact his revenge for what this man had done to Slade's friends. I want to give my husband that chance.

Chapter Seventeen

Ramses Barnett, 1791

I've been away from New York City and my brother for several months now. Since the night Castel showed up and ordered me to stand down. He single-handedly gave Slade the win that night. The win slipped through my fingers when I ran away like a schoolboy coward because the disappointment in Castel's voice cut through me faster than Slade's silver knife. How can my clan ever respect me again when I don't even respect myself anymore?

"The new collection of feeders is in place. We can begin the move back whenever you're ready. Our more experienced clan members are discreetly adding to our numbers, but from other cities to avoid arousing suspicion again. The other businesses you have are thriving and growing more every day." Patrick's daily report is usually positive but rarely cheers me.

"Thank you, Patrick."

The one thing I want more than anything is too far out of my reach. Time and distance have given me a little more perspective. My brother's strength and focus have always been greater than mine, so it's only natural that he'd develop the extended power of the infamous red eyes first. Especially with who his wife is. Even when I flirted with her before they met, that power didn't develop in me, so I shouldn't put all my hope in her being the one to unlock it.

I must keep searching for my immortal love. With having part of the power inside me, courtesy of Castel, I have to believe it'll happen one day. I haven't told Patrick, but that's the main reason why I keep the humans in the cages. The hope that I'll find the one who was made only for me. The one I can't live without, the one who can't live without me, the one who will be my partner for all eternity.

To fill the hole that I haven't been able to fill.

"Ramses, you have a visitor." Patrick interrupted my thoughts.

"Who?"

"Rolland Cleary," he replied. "Do you know him?"

"No. I've never heard of him. Show him to my study. I'll see what Mr. Cleary has to say, then I'll decide if he can leave."

I intentionally let him wait longer than what's considered acceptable in certain social circles. When I entered the room, he showed no sign of irritation or aggravation from being kept waiting. His professional and polite demeanor was intact when he rose to greet me.

"Thank you for seeing me, Mr. Barnett. It's quite rude of me to show up here unannounced and uninvited, but I'm afraid I had no other option. There's a very important business proposition we need to discuss."

"It appears you have me at a disadvantage, Mr. Cleary. It seems you know me well enough to draft a business proposition with my firm, but I don't know you at all. Exactly how is it you know me?"

"My proposition requires a very specific kind of person, with particular skills and abilities most don't have. A person that I have to personally vet before I approach."

His thoughts were hidden from me. Rolland Cleary wasn't a vampire, but he wasn't a human either.

"What kind of person would that be?" My tone challenged him, though I knew exactly what he meant. I only wanted to hear him say it out loud.

Tell me what I am.

"A vampire."

"And what are you, exactly? You're not a

vampire, but you're not a human either."

"I am just a friend who wants to help you with the one thing you've been searching for but has been just out of your reach."

Those words hit me with the force of sledgehammer against my head. How would he know what I've been searching for? He spoke as though he knew exactly what I had been thinking about before his presence was announced. That particular fact made me even more suspicious of him.

"Reveal your true self to me now, or you won't leave me alive."

"No need to get upset. I mean you no harm. I truly want to help you."

"How do you propose to help me? And what do you want in return?"

"Your brother has been watching you very closely. Checking on your movements. Following up on your activities. If he finds out what you're doing, he and Castel will shut your businesses down. Again. I can offer you the protection of my clan. We can form an alliance where you help me and I help you."

"Help you with what?"

"Your clan's ability to find people whose absences don't cause ripples in the pond is more useful than you can imagine. You take the first pick, and let my clan and me have access to the rest. They'll remain in your businesses, everything happens under your direction, and you're still in charge."

"As a skilled negotiator, I know if something sounds too good to be true, it usually is. Why am I getting that feeling right now? Oh yes, because you still haven't told me what you are. And you only want access to my feeders? That's not all you want."

"There may be some unorthodox activities we have planned for them, but nothing that should cause you any concern."

"This is the last time I will ask this before I rip your throat out. What. Are. You?"

With a deep breath and a resigned drop of his shoulders, Rolland finally replied. "I'm a shapeshifter."

"That's not all you are."

"I'm mixed with a vampire."

"That's not possible. Shapeshifter and vampire blood do not mix."

"I was bitten by a vampire, and a strange thing happened when he decided to turn me. Our blood mixed, and my powers changed."

"Changed how?" My curiosity was more than piqued.

He hesitated longer this time, not wanting to share the information he was no doubt waiting to use as leverage against me later. But I wouldn't be denied the full story before I agreed to any type of deal. Especially with a stranger.

"My eyes have flashed red a couple of times. I haven't learned how to fully sustain it yet, but I know others who have. There is a way, and it's not only with finding your immortal love. There's a way to tap into it and unlock it on your own."

"Bullshit."

"Not at all. We'll figure it out together, because neither of us can do it alone. We need each other's help, Ramses. Combining our clans will give us the best of both worlds. We're shapeshifters, so we can easily blend in places where others may find it more difficult."

"Very well, then. I'm in. But know this, Rolland Cleary. If you think you can double-cross me at any time during this partnership, no amount of shapeshifting will save you from me. I will find you, whatever form you're in, and I will kill you in the most unpleasant of ways. You will regret ever having met me should that happen."

"I have no doubt of that, Ramses. It's not something I'm concerned about, though."

Just like that, we moved from strangers to partners. We were united in our quest to find and enslave the humans that society had rejected and forgotten—either as clan members or feeders. My clan had to live, and I reasoned that keeping prisoners was more humane than killing them outright. Our feeders were well cared for and fed good food. That's more than they'd get from anyone else in their lives.

Rolland and his clan of shapeshifters built a house in the mountains not far from my current location. They would sometimes take a few of the feeders out of their cages and into their house. I never questioned Rolland on what they did to them. Part of me was curious to know, but since they always returned the feeder back to the cage the next day unharmed, I assumed the shapeshifters were fucking the ones they liked.

Who am I to judge that? I've done the same thing myself.

The two I brought to my room last night were eager and rigorous with their affections. It doesn't matter who I'm fucking or who I'm feeding on, though. The only scent I smell is the one in my mind. Alea. I smell her in everyone. I taste her blood with every drink. My thirst for her is insatiable. No matter how much I take from someone else, the craving for her never goes away.

"Do I not satisfy you?" the girl last night asked.

"No. But it's not your fault. It's me—I'm broken."

It was the truth—as honest as I can give it. Alea broke me, and when I tasted the first drop of her blood, I felt the fissure inside me crack under the weight of my obsession with her.

"We need to talk about Slade," Rolland announced when he strode into my office unbidden.

"What about him?"

"We need to kill him. He needs to be removed from the equation so we can take over his clan and bring them under our leadership."

"No."

"What do you mean 'no'?"

"How many meanings do you think it has?"

Rolland huffed loudly—exasperated with my sarcasm. "Why would you not want to kill him?"

"Because he's my brother. And I've plotted to kill him before, but my maker stopped me."

"How did he stop you?"

"He showed up and ordered me to stand down. I had no choice but to obey him."

"No, you didn't have to, Ramses. You can assert your own will and your dominance. That breaks the creator's hold over you."

"You're serious?"

Understanding dawned in his expression. "They never told you that, did they?"

"No. They didn't."

"So they could keep controlling you, Ramses. You're destined for greatness. We can take over his clan. Are you ready?"

"We can't. Not until we've unlocked the secret of the red-eyed vampire."

"Why do you say that?"

"Because Slade is one, and his strength and powers are beyond compare. We'd never be able to stand against him."

Rolland looked somewhat surprised, but only in the way that his suspicions had finally been confirmed. I suddenly questioned the intentions of my odd new friend. Though several weeks had passed with him and his clan literally at my side, when I revealed Slade's secret, Rolland seemed different.

"You still love your brother after all his deceit. I can sense it."

"I do," I admitted. "He is my brother. He may have kept things from me, but he has always been the one to look after me."

"Was he looking after you when he stole your woman from you?"

"He didn't. She wasn't mine to steal," I denied. "Wait. How did you know that?"

"People talk. Your men talk. It is known throughout our clans. They can't see you as weak, Ramses. You have to show them you're the leader, or they won't follow you. Just as you don't have to follow Castel any longer."

His argument made sense, yet his words stirred dread in me. The clan war had not ended well in my favor, and yet he urged me to start another one and take over my brother's place.

"I do need to prove I'm worthy and establish my rightful place as the leader since I'm the eldest."

"Yes, you do. There's no need to start an all-out

clan war. This time, it just needs to be you against Slade. Confront him and expose his weakness. Then we can form an attack."

"His only weakness is Alea," I replied absently. "She is the only one who can bring him to his knees."

"Then we need to take her and put him in a place of vulnerability."

"That would only make him stronger. I've learned that firsthand."

"Not if we do it right," Rolland replied. "Leave that to me. There are ways."

"I don't want my brother killed, Rolland. Or Alea, for that matter."

"I can't promise Slade's safety, but I have no qualms with promising his wife's safety. She'll just be the bait to get him where we want him. If he cooperates, we don't have to kill him. If he fights, I can't say what will happen to him."

Regardless of what's happened between Slade and me, I didn't appreciate hearing those words from another man. I haven't been the best brother to him, but I'm sure as hell not going to allow another man to kill my brother. That's not something I shared with Rolland, though.

After Rolland left, I called for Patrick. I needed my friend's input.

"What do you think of our business associate?" I asked.

"I don't trust him, Ramses. I understand he says

he's a shapeshifter and vampire mix, so my senses will be off-kilter because he's an unusual breed. But I know there's more to him than he's showing us."

"Why do you say that?"

"He can read our thoughts but hide his from us. I've never met anyone who can do both."

"Can you hide your thoughts from him?"

"Only with strong concentration. I can feel him scratching at the wall, trying to get in, though."

"Perhaps it's time to part ways with him and his clan. We can cancel this entire plan and go back to our original plan."

"Be careful, Ramses. I don't think he'll give this up without a fight."

Alea Barnett, 1791

Telling Slade I found the vampire hunter was not a pleasant conversation for me. The red flashed in his eyes as soon as the words left my mouth.

"You what?" His voice was low and tight. He was holding on to his temper by a thread.

"I found him. I know where he's staying. And he was sleeping during the day. He must believe all the folklore that we only move around during the night. That tells me he's not as experienced as he thinks he is."

"Alea, you weren't supposed to go looking for him alone. What if he'd woken while you were in there? He's faster than you're giving him credit for. What if he'd killed you?"

"Slade, I'm fine. I'm not as helpless as you seem to think I am. He had no idea I was there. In fact, I could've killed him on the spot, but I wanted you to have the pleasure."

Slade walked away several steps and stopped with his back to me. "I know you're not helpless. You're strong and fearless. I'm the one who's losing my grip. I'm sorry—my fear of losing you is affecting my ability to be objective."

"You never have to be sorry for showing your love for me. Let me help you feel better about my skills with you nearby to step in and assist if I need you." I watched his body language to gauge his reaction. I understood his anxiousness all too well. I can barely manage my own craving for him.

"How do you suggest we do this?"

"We wait until he leaves tonight and follow him. When we reach an isolated area, I'll incapacitate him, and you can kill him for what he did to your friends."

"You'll incapacitate him?"

"Trust me, my love. It'll be fine. I will be fine."

"Okay. Thomas and I will both be there to make sure you're safe. That's not up for negotiation."

"Agreed. You and Thomas can both be there as my bodyguards. I won't argue."

Slade, Thomas, and I set out at dusk to wait

for the elusive hunter to emerge from his tiny apartment. He was a handsome man, approximately thirty years old. His hair was as black as coal, and his eyes were brown like Slade's. He was taller than most men I know and physically fit. His long legs carried him with confidence, and his stride had purpose. He would not go down without a fight—that much I was sure of. The element of surprise was on my side, though.

I moved ahead of him with ease and waited around the corner for him to catch up to me. When I heard him approach, I walked out of the shadows and into his path. While I wrung my hands and turned around in slow circles, he approached me.

"Miss? What are you doing out here alone at this time?"

"I'm new here and got turned around when I went for a walk. I don't know where I am or where I'm even supposed to be. All I remember is the building had a beautiful fountain in front."

"I believe I know exactly where you're supposed to be. I'll walk you. It's not safe for you to walk out here alone."

He was so nice and very polite. It was hard to imagine he was the same man who was a self-proclaimed vampire hunter. But, of course, I knew he was. We walked for a few steps until we were in deep shadows, shielded by the tall buildings on both sides of the street.

"Thank you for walking with me. Where are you from?"

"A small village in Spain, originally. But I've moved around a lot. I don't really have a home anymore."

"You don't have any family left in your Spanish village?"

"No one is left in that village." He paused for a heartbeat. "Someone, or something, killed everyone. Took everything in my life from me. Now I travel and hunt for those monsters who killed my family and friends."

"What kind of monsters? What do you mean?" I withdrew from his proximity and looked at him suspiciously.

"You wouldn't believe me if I told you." He sounded defeated. "But there are evil people in this world who do unspeakable things. I'm just doing what I can to help keep as many humans safe as I can. I've made some mistakes along the way, but my intentions are honorable."

"Mistakes? So you've missed some of these monsters?"

"Yes, I've missed some. And I've mislabeled some people as monsters when they weren't. That's my biggest regret."

"What's your name? I believe we completely missed our introductions."

"I'm Leo Michel. And you are?"

"My name is Alea Barnett." I paused my steps and turned to face him directly when I spoke.

"Very nice to meet you, Miss Alea," he replied politely and bowed slightly.

It was then that I made my move. He wasn't ready for me, my speed, or my strength. When he realized what had happened, he struggled against my firm hold, but his writhing was pointless. His muscular arms were useless against my dainty hands. The silver blade in his pocket might as well have been in his desolate Spanish village for all the good it was to him.

I turned him so that his back was against my front, his arms were securely behind his back, and my cheek was close to his cheek.

"Allow me to finish introducing myself. My name is Mrs. Slade Barnett, and you tried to kill my husband after murdering his human friends. Now that you've made the foolish mistake of bringing your job here, I'll allow my husband to exact revenge on behalf of his friends."

Slade emerged from thin air directly in front of us. His eyes were red, and inherent danger radiated from his presence. The murderous expression he wore conveyed his plans for the unwanted visitor.

"Wait," Thomas commanded as he made his presence known. "I've seen his future. We should change him instead of kill him."

Slade's already chilling expression changed to a

devious smile. "What a perfect suggestion, Thomas. Rather than kill the hunter, we'll change him into the very thing he hunts."

Leo started to object but barely made a sound before Slade bit him and drained his blood.

"Now you're too weak to fight." Slade slit open his wrist and forced the blood into Leo's mouth. Leo didn't have to swallow willingly—the infected blood slid down his throat from his lack of strength to prevent it. "Welcome to the family, Leo."

Chapter Eighteen

Slade Barnett, 1792

I've tried to stay away from Ramses as much as possible over the last few months. It does no good for me to visit his mountain home. Every time I have, the rage fills me and makes me want to tear his entire world down. The last time I was there, he was rebuilding his cages to hold humans against their will. He always takes one more step toward revealing us to the world.

But it's both dangerous and foolish to think he isn't up to no good, so I forced myself to check on him again.

And I did not like what I found at all.

Rolland Cleary has joined Ramses in the mountains. They've built their own cozy little community deep in the forest, away from the prying eyes of others. Rolland's clan was with him, and they're actively working with Ramses's clan. The fact of the matter was I had to find out what they were up to, why they'd joined forces. I hovered around different members to listen to their private conversations in an attempt to gather information on their plans.

Rolland had offered to help me infiltrate Ramses's clan and stop his insanity. But it was an offer I didn't feel comfortable accepting. The man was obviously hiding something, and I wasn't willing to put my wife and my clan in harm's way. Now it appears he has found a new home with others who aren't quite right. He joined Ramses's clan.

Was their plan to mount a joint attack on my clan?

Just when I thought life could become routine and normal. Well, as normal as normal can be for a family of vampires. But then, Ramses never has been ordinary, and he never allowed our lives to become conventional or routine. Since he hadn't changed in the slightest, I had to play the role of the adult and nanny to my older brother. Even though I'd rather spend my spare time with my wife, I was forced to divide it between her and spying on my brother.

Moving around their compound made one thing abundantly clear. The lower level members of the clan haven't been given any information at all regarding the plans they have in place. That means the plans are big—and the leaders have gone to extreme measures to keep them completely secret. They weren't taking any chances with the weaker members having knowledge of their underhanded schemes.

I moved on to another area where multiple clan members had collected, speaking in hushed tones. I could only hope I was moving up the chain to someone who could provide any information on what they'd been doing, what they were working on, and what they were planning.

"Rolland said to make sure your assigned men are trained and ready to go at a moment's notice."

"When is it happening?"

"He hasn't said. We won't know until it's time to make our move. I think it'll be soon, though."

"What do you know about Slade? I've heard Ramses's clan members talk about his abilities."

"I've only heard what you've heard. No one wants to take him on one-on-one. Some say he has some kind of rare power."

Their conversation confirmed my suspicions. They're plotting something against me. Only Rolland knows what that is and when it'll happen. Until then, a lot more of my time will be spent in the mountains, trying to identify what I can do to stop whatever is coming before it's too late.

I moved again and kept a watchful eye for any movement. Two men emerged from Rolland's house. Their eyes were kept straightforward, focused on their destination. Determination was set in their expressions. There was no mistaking the gait of men on a mission. These were two men who had information, and I needed it.

I followed them into the forest, away from the rest of the clan, and watched as they fed on several large animals. Hour after hour, they moved from place to place, stalking their prey and pouncing when they had the animal cornered exactly where they wanted it. They were building their strength without causing suspicion in the city by creating more missing persons. They were preparing their bodies for something major, for a fight to the death.

Was that fight to the death intended to be with me?

If Ramses and Rolland are at the helm, the answer is most definitely yes.

When they'd finally had enough to drink, the sun was rising. I realized I'd been away from home all night. Alea would be beside herself with worry over me, followed by incredible anger and hurt when I returned home and explained my absence. How would I explain neglecting to tell my wife I've been spying on my brother who doesn't live anywhere near us?

That conversation should go very well.

The two men I'd been following and watching stopped walking without warning and looked at each other. Then they burst out laughing.

"We know you've been following us. Rolland told us you would. He also just told me to tell you he hopes you enjoyed our little show. His plan worked better than he thought it would."

"Hurry home now."

Alea Barnett, 1792

With Thomas working in the office with Slade, my assistance wasn't needed as much. While growing the business was a good thing, not going into the office left too much time on my hands. Hours and hours of nothing to do, forcing me to find anything to hold my attention. I looked forward to the hour when Slade normally walked through the door. He's been later some days than others, but then he'd also been earlier at times. But when Slade didn't return home anywhere near his normal time, my first thought was he'd been held over by a client or possibly had fed without me. Either way, a word to alert me would've been the polite thing to do.

The more time passed, the more concerned I became. He'd been venturing off more frequently lately, but never for so long. He didn't bother to share where he'd gone with me, but I knew Ramses still consumed his thoughts. It was only natural he'd want some time alone to process his thoughts and work through his frustrations. My main concern of not knowing where he'd gone was his safety. One vampire hunter had already turned up and Slade changed him, but there are more out there.

A knock at the door alarmed me since I wasn't expecting visitors. When our servants brought my unexpected guest into the parlor, I could barely speak because of the shock.

"Sean?"

"It's me, Alea. I'm sorry to show up unannounced, but it took me most of the day to locate you and I didn't want to wait another minute to see you again."

"How can this be? I was told you were dead."

"Umm—no. I am alive and well, as you can see. Would it be inappropriate for me to wrap my arms around you and hug you as tightly as I can?"

"No, that wouldn't be inappropriate at all!" I leapt into his embrace, so happy to see my friend again. To learn he wasn't executed, contrary to what Ramses said.

Sean wrapped his arms around my waist, and my arms went around his neck. He squeezed and I pretended to be crushed, though I was the one who had to take care not to hurt him. Through all of this, my happiness over having my friend back was all I could think about.

"I've missed you, Alea."

"I've missed you, too. You have no idea. When I was told you'd been killed, I was so heartbroken. I still can't believe you're here."

He released me, and we sat together. "Alea, you look absolutely radiant. Marriage agrees with you in every way."

"It definitely does. I can't wait for you to meet Slade. I've told him all about you."

Sean smiled warmly. "You'll always be the one who got away from me."

He asked a lot of questions about my life, and we talked for a couple of hours. He asked me about married life, Slade, and the differences of living in America. I shared as much as I could without giving away our family secret. Sean soaked up every word, as thrilled to see me as I was him. The miracle of my oldest friend sitting next to me was blindingly beautiful.

When he stood to leave, I realized how long we'd been talking, but Slade still hadn't returned home. I hid my concern and escorted Sean to the door.

"How long are you staying?"

"I have no plans to return to London. I'll be here for the foreseeable future." He kissed my cheek, hugged me again, and stepped outside.

"I'm thrilled to hear that, Sean. You are welcome here anytime. You must come back soon and meet my husband. He'll be sorry to hear he missed you tonight."

"Good night, Alea. I'll see you again very soon."

I returned to the settee and began journaling the return of my friend Sean, though my mind kept wandering back to Slade.

A noise outside the front door drew my attention. Concerned Slade had been injured by a hunter, I rushed to the door to check.

"Sean? Did you forget something?"

"Yes. I forgot you."

"What do you mean?"

Before I could process his intent, several men rushed me and threw a silver chain mail over my head, effectively rendering my power useless. They picked me up and sprinted away from the city, moving north toward the mountains in the upstate area.

When we reached the hideaway, Sean put me in a cell with silver bars.

"Here's your journal. You can finish writing about us now. It's very touching to read how much you missed me." He pushed my journal and writing pen through the bars, then changed his appearance before my eyes.

"Rolland."

"Did you honestly think I was your old friend Sean? Oh, I'm sorry, dear. Ramses didn't lie to you. Sean died some time ago. But I appreciate all the information you shared about Slade. It'll help me tremendously when he shows up here to get you, and I use it against him to kill him. You'll have a first-row seat to watch."

"Was this your plan all along?"

"Of course. I just had to take a more indirect route to get here. You and Slade wouldn't accept my offer, but Ramses did."

"Why? What do you hope to gain from this?"

"His blood. The *maestro rosso* in him is stronger than in any other vampire I've encountered. If I take his blood, it'll complete what's inside me and then I'll possess the power. Like everything else in this world, it all depends on who the strongest is. Do you have any last words you'd like me to convey to your husband?"

"Yes. Tell him I said to rip your throat out and save it as a trophy for me when he takes me home later. Because that's exactly what's going to happen when he finds out you've taken me. You'll wish you'd never met anyone named Barnett by the time this night is over. You want to know who the strongest is? You won't actually get to meet him— because you'll never even see him coming."

Chapter Nineteen

Ramses Barnett, 1792

Rolland's words keep replaying in my mind, a taunting chant of how something so simple yet imperative was kept from me. The more I think about it, the angrier I become. How could I have been so blind all these years? I've been played for the fool in so many ways by the two men who were supposed to be my family.

My brother and my creator.

Slade and Castel have lied to me and hidden crucial information from me. They've intentionally held me back from being the most powerful vampire I could possibly be. The first important piece of information was, of course, the legend of and the secret behind the red-eyed powers. Finding that out the way I did was bad enough. Knowing they conspired together against me was worse.

But I've only recently learned yet another element of the life I've lived for more than a hundred years. All this time, I could've broken the control Castel has over me by simply asserting my own will against his commands. When he showed up at the park that night and ordered me to make my clan retreat, I didn't have to obey him. I wasn't required to bend to his will. I've always conformed to his directives because his power is so strong, and that was what he'd taught me to do. Now I clearly see that Castel and Slade intentionally held me back to keep me under their thumbs. The only explanation is they're both jealous of me because they know I'm the one who was destined for greatness, but they wanted it all for themselves instead.

My previous plans failed partly because of them, but I have to accept the bulk of the blame. Going after Alea in my brother's house without the full power awakened inside me was utterly foolish. I knew going in Slade's strength exceeded mine, even under normal circumstances. Had they told me about the additional powers I could've developed and mastered by now, I have no doubt the outcome would've been very different.

That action created an immediate reaction with outcomes and consequences I never could've predicted. The power that awakened in Slade and the conflict that erupted between the two of us summoned Castel to our location. As our creator, he felt the tremors of discord in his family. He heard the murderous thoughts in our heads. The only thing he could do besides kill us, or rather, kill me, was to stop us from going any further than we already had.

I examined all the facts and relived every interaction before my next move became clear to me. When I realized, after much deliberation, what I had to do, a huge weight fell from my shoulders and my path became evident.

Patrick and I took an unscheduled trip to a tiny village located on the northern coast of Sardinia. It's completely ironic that the name of the town is Castelsardo, since it's not named after Castel. But he most likely chose it out of his vanity and pride anyway. As point after point occurred to me, I had to wonder how I missed all the obvious clues for so long.

We arrived at Castel's beachfront mansion unannounced and unexpected, just the way I'd planned. There were no sentinels standing guard. No rabid dogs to protect their master. My exact thought as I entered his home, my home during my early vampire years, was how poetic it would be for my vampire father to die in the same place where he changed my real father, and then watched as my father killed my mother.

My revenge has been a long time coming.

Patrick and I drifted through the palatial beachfront home, silently searching for Castel. Each room I passed through held too many memories from my younger years as a vampire. They all hit me at once—the good and the bad mixing together until my mind was a jumbled mess. Scenes of Castel and me together, him patiently teaching me all I needed to know.

The view from the veranda outside the kitchen evoked the next memory. Slade and I left together on a hunting mission, practicing our vampire skills in another coastal town on the mainland. We moved our stalking grounds as far away from our lair as possible to avoid drawing unwanted attention. Our village was much too small to feed on anyone and not cause suspicion, risking being beheaded or burned at the stake

The next room was the grand banquet hall. When Slade and I had mastered our gifts, Castel held a masquerade ball for us. His clan brought humans in from all corners of the world for us to feast on in celebration. Castel was so proud of us that night. He boasted to all of his vampire friends from distant clans about how well his sons had learned the vampire ways. The admiration he held for us was never kept a secret.

In the library next, scenes from my time alone with Castel flashed before my eyes. He spent hours with me, going page by page through the many books he owned, introducing me to more knowledge than any human could fathom. His patience with my questions never waned even once. "We have plenty of time, my son," he'd said. "Ask all the questions you want." When I was ready, he'd switch to teaching me other languages to help me blend in wherever my travels would take me.

The great room presented a different memory entirely. The sharp pain that shot through my chest as the events replayed brought me to my knees. There, in front of me, I saw my beloved mother and my father as plainly as I saw Patrick standing beside me. It was that day all over again. The day Castel changed Slade and me. The day he changed my father into the monster that killed my mother, the one person who'd always loved me for me— flaws and achievements alike. Then I watched as Castel killed my father before I lost consciousness.

I closed my eyes. I couldn't bear to watch it happen a second time in one lifetime. Losing my mother was something I'd never recovered from. Seeing my father murder the woman we both loved more than our own lives haunted me for a century. Reliving that again would be unbearable.

"Look again, Ramses," a familiar voice urged gently.

"No." My reply was adamant and resolute.

"It's not as you remember, my son. You need to

watch and understand the truth."

Against my better judgment, I opened my eyes and steadied myself to relive the day my whole family died. It was by far the worst day of my life.

Castel and three other vampires from his clan carried the four of us in their arms as they drifted through the wall and into the great room.

"Quickly. Lay them here on the floor. We're almost out of time," Castel commanded.

My eyes drifted to my mother's face. It had been so long since I'd seen her, but there she was again. She was already so pale her skin was almost translucent. Her breaths were slow, labored, and shallow. She was fading so fast. My gaze darted over to where the mortal version of myself lay on the cold, marble floor. Even then, I was calling to my mother, begging her to hold on.

"Mother, keep breathing. Do not give up. I beg of you, sir. Please help her first."

Castel was kneeling beside my father and looked up when he heard my plea. My voice was so weak when I asked him to help her first, it was barely audible. At the time, I thought I was yelling at the top of my lungs.

Castel and the others exchanged knowing glances. "I will try my best to help her."

He finished sharing his blood with my father, allowing him time to go through the change as Castel checked on my mother. He knelt over her and inhaled a long breath, taking in her scent first. Then he closed his eyes and bowed his head.

"I'm sorry, my boy. She's already gone. I cannot bring her back now." His voice was thick with remorse. Then he moved to Slade next.

"Your brother is very sick. Much more so than you are. I will help him before it's too late. You've lost enough today."

From my kneeling position, I watched the events of that day replay as if I were an outsider to the entire scene. Castel's fangs extended, ripped into his own flesh, and exposed more of his blood. It dripped into Slade's mouth, forcing him to either swallow or drown in it. I watched the muscles in his neck as they barely moved, forcing the life-giving liquid down as best as his sickly body would allow.

By the time Castel moved to me, my father had completed his mortal death and his rebirth as a vampire. Castel again opened his artery and held his wrist over my mouth. The toxic nature of vampire blood stops the heart from beating. The pain is excruciating as the internal organs cease to work and the change begins. My mortal body began to convulse as it went through the stages of dying.

In the scene before me, I watched as I fought against losing consciousness due to the pain, keeping my eyes fixed on my mother even when I started to drift away. My father's wails of pain drew my attention away from the younger Ramses on the floor, and I observed his actions with rapt attention.

He had been changed into a full vampire—but his dead heart was still connected to my mother. In the blink of an eye, he was at her side, gathering her into his arms and hiding his face in the crook of her neck. He rocked back and forth, wailing inconsolably. His only coherent words were repeated over and over.

"Not without you. Not without you."

My father looked up at Castel, tears of blood streaked down his face. "You promised me, Castel. You gave me your word."

"But your sons..." Castel objected.

"You gave me your word!"

Castel nodded, his shoulders drooped, and his steps were slow when he walked to the far wall. He lifted the silver sword from its resting place and begrudgingly returned to my father.

"You promised, Castel. It's what I want you to do. I can't live an eternity without her."

Castel placed his hand on my father's shoulder. Remorse filled his face. "I am sorry, my friend."

"Take care of my boys. They're your sons now."

"I give you my word. Your sons will be treated as my own," Castel assured him. With that, my father drew my mother's lifeless body close to his chest again and closed his eyes. Castel's swing made a clean cut through my father's neck.

The other clan members carried my parents

to the funeral pyre outside and stood solemnly by until the fire burned itself out.

The vision cleared from the room, but I couldn't move from my position on my knees. "All these years, I've had recurring visions of you turning my father into a monster that killed my mother. And then you killed my father—but not for the reason I just witnessed."

"Had I realized that's what you believed happened, I would've shared my memory with you much sooner. Why did you never tell me, Ramses?"

It was well past time to be completely honest—with myself.

"Because I loved you, Castel. I loved you like a son loves his father. I admired you and wanted to be exactly like you. And if that were true, if you had caused my parents' death, I didn't want to know. Not really."

"But you've been conflicted all this time. Torn between not wanting to love me and wishing you could hate me. Feeling guilty for being associated in any way with the one who took your parents from you was bad enough, but loving and admiring that man drove you to madness..." Castel replied, filling in the words I still couldn't say.

"Yes." I dropped my head in shame.

"You've resisted me for a long time, Ramses. If you'll open your mind to me, I can help repair some of the damage caused to your psyche over the years.

Let me give you the peace you deserve."

"What I deserve," I repeated solemnly. "I don't deserve anything good after what I've done to you. To Slade. To Alea. I deserve wrath and vengeance."

"You're my son. Accept this gift from me. The rest will have to be worked out with Slade and Alea."

I nodded in agreement, accepting his offer and a little reprieve from the mental anguish and guilt I'd carried for far too long. Like a soothing balm covering raw hide, his healing touch removed the years of built-up scars and calluses in my mind. When he finished, I actually felt genuine feelings once again.

The time had come for me to return home and face my own shortcomings without blaming everyone else in my life for my own actions. My arrival back home was punctuated by a presence I longed for daily. She was nearby—Alea was here. But why? She would never willingly leave Slade, that much I already knew. There could only be one reason why she'd be in this area, and the ramifications of that reason would be insurmountable. My clan partner must be more insane than I'd realized if he'd kidnapped Alea and held her prisoner here.

Slade would be unstoppable in his quest to retrieve her. The war he'd bring to our doorsteps would be a one-sided massacre. With his power, he could obliterate his enemies and they'd never even know he'd been there. Rolland had no idea what chain of events he'd just set into motion with his latest move.

I, for one, would not be a party to his madness.

While Rolland engaged his clan, Patrick used his power to hide my telepathic message and I issued a silent command to mine to leave as quickly as possible and not return until they heard from me again. If nothing else, I'd protect my people from the lunatic who'd taken over—and for once, that lunatic wasn't me. I stole into the basement of Rolland's house while he was busy strategically placing his men in different locations in the forest. He'd been busy while Patrick and I were in Italy.

A brand new cell had been constructed, complete with silver bars, just for Alea. She paced back and forth inside, turning on her heel just before she touched the bars and clutching her journal tightly in her hand. She knew I was there, but she refused to look at me.

"Alea." Remorse filled my tone—from helping to put her in this position to begin with to being unable to free her from the silver prison.

"My husband will be here soon. If you want to live past the next few minutes, I suggest you do the same as you commanded your clan to do. Get away from me." Her eyes flashed red, resembling an uncontrollable fire burning rampant deep inside. The longer she stared at me, the hotter it burned, and the more I felt the flames leap out and strike me.

"I'll go," I agreed. "I'm sorry, Alea. For all of this."

Chapter Twenty

Ramses Barnett, 1792

I watched from the sidewalk when Slade returned home to his empty house. His expression confirmed he knew she wasn't there before he stepped foot inside. But he held on to a sliver of hope that he was wrong. He wasn't. When he fully realized it, a side of my brother emerged that I never knew existed in him. He was a crazed man, his need for her driving him to madness. His obsession with her feeding his panic. He must have torn every room apart looking for her. Screaming her name.

But he knew. He knew he'd been played for a complete fool.

I knew I should've left before he came back out of his house. I should've flown back to the rendezvous point and waited for my clan. But I couldn't do it.

I couldn't miss the most pivotal moment in the entire game. The moment when my perfect brother completely lost his mind and joined the ranks of the insane.

When he burst through the second-floor window, I felt his power shooting out of every pore in his body. His eyes were red, of course, but that wasn't the only thing. All of him appeared to glow red—from the top of his head to the bottom of his feet. Through his clothes and his shoes, like a large ball of fire streaking through the sky.

He was terrifying. And he was going straight for Rolland, just as Rolland had intended. To his deathtrap.

"Slade! Wait!" The words were out of my mouth before I could stop them.

He turned his fiery gaze on me, murder raging in his eyes. In an instant, he'd grabbed me and lifted me with one arm. "What have you done?"

"Slade, listen to me. I'm trying to help. But I need your help first."

"Talk. If I don't like what I hear, I'll rip your head off with my bare hands."

"Rolland came to me and wanted to join clans for our mutual benefit and protection. I agreed, but then later I changed my mind.

"When I tried to break the agreement, he threatened to kill you and Alea. So I've stayed put and bit my tongue for as long as I can take it. I wasn't at the house while he had you distracted and he was abducting Alea. I've only just returned from a trip to Castel's and learned Rolland had gone through with his plan.

"He took her back there and put her in a silver cell. You won't be able to get close to it without losing your powers and risking your life."

"Are you trying to tell me not to go get my wife?" he growled, his voice rumbling through the street and the buildings like an earthquake.

"No. I know better than that. I'm saying if you rush in there headfirst, it'll be a dead end for both of you."

"Why are you trying to help me now?"

"I need you to get me out of this pact with Rolland. He's taking over my clan. He's changing my vampires to shapeshifter hybrids. I believe he'll kill me after he's killed you and Alea."

"Looking out for yourself again, I see."

"Are you going to help me or not, Slade?"

"No. I'm going to help my wife. Stay here. If I see you anywhere near the houses, you're a dead man. I'm going to bring my wife home now."

With that last threat, he disappeared—not even a red streak was left behind.

The next time I return to my mountain home, the entire area will look vastly different after he finishes razing the houses. I waited in the city like I promised I would. Slade's threat to kill me wasn't just idle words. They were his oath and his honor—and he'd uphold them. So I roamed the streets I used to call home, reliving the sights and scents from a better time in my life. A time that held meaning and purpose. And fun.

It'd been so long since I'd just had fun.

But that had to wait until Slade returned and I was certain Rolland was out of my life.

A few hours later, I felt his presence again. The anticipation of the whole situation was killing me. I've never been a patient man, but waiting to see which super-monster would win the battle was excruciating.

Even with my impatience at an all-time high, I took my time walking back to Slade's house. If anything went wrong, my brother would not be glad to see me, even more so than usual. When I arrived back at their house at last, I saw Slade and Alea embrace in the second-floor hole in the wall that was once a window.

They felt my presence and joined me on the street. "I'm glad you're both back safe and sound."

"Rolland is dead." Slade's voice held no brotherly love. No forgiveness. Nothing but contempt for me. "So are all of the hybrids."

"I'm actually very glad to hear that. Thank you for taking care of this problem."

"It wasn't for you," Slade replied.

"How did you get her out of the cell?"

"I made one of the hybrids do it."

"Your subtle nudges, huh?"

He didn't reply. He didn't smile or acknowledge my friendly gesture in any way.

"Ramses, we're going to come to a truce right here, right now. It'll be sworn in blood oaths and will hold for all time. If you don't agree to the terms, our clan will destroy you and yours." Alea spoke with fierceness and directness.

"What are your terms?"

"They're very simple, really." She handed me a sheet of parchment from the journal she'd had with her in the cell. The rules were clearly outlined for me.

1. *Human prisoners are not allowed. Willing human feeders are allowed if they are properly cared for. No cages or cells.*

2. *Do not do anything to call any unnecessary attention to vampires.*

3. *Do not instigate or participate in any plans for coups.*

4. *Any vampire can join either clan of his or her choice. Once a choice has been made, the clan will expect full loyalty.*

5. *There is no mixing of species or forming alliances of any kind.*

"Do you agree to these terms?" Alea asked.

"Yes. I agree."

She pulled a silver blade out and handed it to

me. "Then seal it with your blood oath. If you break this oath, it will result in your death."

I took the blade and sliced my palm open. I squeezed the blood onto the parchment and swore my oath before them. Alea and Slade did the same, ending our clan war.

"This truce will last as long as you allow it. But you won't be allowed back into our lives for any reason. Take your clan. Live by the code. Keep the peace. But keep your distance." Slade produced a map of the city. "We will both keep our clans within our boundaries."

"Fine."

Slade and Alea turned and walked away, but there was one more question I needed answered.

"Slade." He turned and looked at me. "Is it true I could've broken Castel's control over me at any time?"

"Yes. That is true. You've always had the power to take control. But you've always lacked the discipline to regulate yourself."

Slade Barnett, 1792

The recent events would be an extraordinary story, if anyone besides me had survived to tell the tale, that is. When I realized Rolland had Alea, nothing else in the world mattered. Not my business. Not my home. Not my life. My sole focus was my wife and her safety. She was fierce and strong herself, but I couldn't take any chances. Castel had urged us to allow the monster within to live and breathe on its own, and that's exactly what I intended to do.

The rage within me built to unimaginable levels before I simply let go and allowed the red master and myself to merge into one person—for good. The feeling of ultimate power and complete control made my entire body tingle with excitement. By truly giving myself over to the darkness inside, I unlocked gifts I never knew were possible. Never even imagined a vampire possessing. Suggestive nudges had given way to total mind control. Flying had morphed into transporting to a location by simply thinking. I could disintegrate others with a flick of my hand or a focused glare.

But the most incredible of the new gifts was being impervious to silver. For all I knew, I was the only vampire who couldn't be killed. I'd truly become immortal thanks to the amazing, frightening new power.

When I arrived at Rolland's house, my enhanced senses told me where every member of the clan was hidden and where my wife was being kept. I walked through their encampment, blatantly in the open, daring anyone to challenge me. Not that I'd planned to allow any of them to get out alive, but giving them the illusion of hope only to dash it was more satisfying than killing them outright. Nevertheless, that's exactly what happened. When I freed Alea from her cell, the silver broke as easily as dried clay under my touch.

I purposely kept that part from Ramses when he asked how I'd released her from the silver bars. If he knew, his quest to possess the enhanced powers would never end. His obsession with it would only grow and destroy him—whether by my hand or someone else's. He'd heard rumors about the *maestro rosso* protecting vampires from silver and only wanted to verify if they were true.

Taking Rolland's head was especially gratifying. He didn't get the courtesy of being destroyed quickly like the others. When I removed his head from his body, I did so with my own hands and nothing else. By the time I'd finished with the shapeshifting-hybrid clan, the area appeared to be truly hell on earth, with the epicenter of Lucifer's arrival being where Rolland's house once stood. Not one brick or scrap of wood remained.

Alea and I left side by side, hand in hand, as it should be. As it will always be—at the head of the clan Thomas has been building for us. Under our guidance, the future of our species will be guaranteed and our reach will be far and wide. On our return trip home, a glimpse into the future alerted me of what's to come—the ones who have been cowardly and false will reveal themselves again one day. When that day comes, we'll be ready. And they'll be sorry.

Epilogue

Ramses Barnett, Current Day

That scent haunts me, like the ghosts of my past. Like the regrets I've lived with for centuries and still can't shake to this very day. There are so many things I should want to change, if only I could somehow magically transport myself back in time while retaining my present knowledge.

But if I did that, if I changed the regrets I know I *should* want to change, I wouldn't be exactly where I am today. I couldn't take that chance even if a magic genie emerged from a lamp and granted my three wishes. The one person I've searched over a lifetime for is here, in New York City, right now.

Her scent disappeared at the street corner, and like an obsessive stalker, I've waited at that same spot for weeks, hoping she'll return, banking on the chance she frequents that specific area. My rational side warns me not to get my hopes up. It reminds me how many tourists visit the city on any given day and how she could be one of them. Add to that fact there are five boroughs and millions of people packed into a relatively small area, and the odds of finding her greatly diminish.

She literally could be anywhere, I realize that.

But my instincts tell me otherwise. They demand that I search for her and make her mine.

After all these years of being estranged from my brother, I can say I've learned one thing for certain. Family means everything. When I find her, I can't use my powers to force her to want me in return. She has to choose me of her own free will. She has to want me with her own carnal desires. She has to willingly give herself to me before we can both be free.

The only regret from my past I would change if I could is losing my brother. I can't forgive myself for the despicable crimes I committed against him. Over my entire life—mortal and immortal combined—he always acted with my well-being in mind. Even the things he kept from me were to protect me from myself. It's taken me far too long to realize and accept that plain and simple fact.

Even after all the mistakes I've made and the impulsive actions that could've gotten us both killed, he still found ways to protect me. At every turn, I've repaid his loyalty with disloyalty. He showed kindness, and I responded with hatred. He always had my back, but I repeatedly stabbed his.

He only wanted the best for me.

I only wanted everything he had.

Had there been any other way to accomplish my goal, I would've gladly taken that path. His absence in my life creates a black hole of despair to this day, despite the truce we brokered between our clans. A truce that has held for over two hundred years.

That truce will break when I find her—my immortal love. The secrets I made in the dark will come to light. The clans of New York City will once again be at each other's throats. I'll have more regrets to add to my collection, but at least they'll have a purpose behind them if I have her. I'll have to answer for what I've done, for what I've hidden all these years, and for the enemy I've lied to protect all these years.

I've spent enough time waiting and watching, hoping to have my soul restored and my mind eased. My next move will be to mobilize my troops to find her. There are so many more advantages to being an immortal in the twenty-first century. Cell phones, Internet access, fake identification, and clan members established in key positions create the ultimate army with the most advanced methods to stay ahead of the rest. Every last resource at my disposal will be tasked with locating this one woman.

The only woman who can unlock my inner power.

The only one who is my immortal love.

ACKNOWLEDGEMENTS

First and foremost, I want to thank my Lord and Savior for His continued forgiveness of a sinner.

To my husband: I love you! Thank you for your unwavering support and love!

To my betas: You are the best. Thank you for being my beta readers, my sounding boards, my biggest supporters, and the all-around best people in the world. Love all of you!

To my readers: Thank you for taking a chance on an indie author and all your support. I love hearing from everyone, so stop by my page and say hello.

To my assistant: Tabitha Charisse, thank you for all your help and support. I love you, girl! You help keep me sane and allow me to make you crazy with my ideas. By the way, you can never leave me. I know where you live. ☺

To special friends: AM Madden, thank you for reading, re-reading, and giving feedback every step of the way—and all the therapeutic chats about every funny and frustrating aspect! Lots of love for you!

Michelle Dare, thank you for all the late night inappropriate meme wars, sharing my love of sarcastic humor, and keeping me in stitches. Love you!

To the bloggers: None of this would be possible without your help, support, and tireless pimping. I love everyone in this great group of people. I can't name one without naming everyone because you've all been so helpful and wonderful friends.

To my editor: Lisa Hollett, with Silently Correcting Your Grammar, thank you for all the help and support you give at all hours of the day and night. I love how you get my sarcasm and the grammatical rules I refuse to follow. But I think you're out of commas now, so you'd better stock up! ☺

ABOUT THE AUTHOR

A.D. Justice is happily married to her husband of more than twenty-five years. They have two sons together and enjoy a wide variety of outdoor activities. A.D. has a full-time job by day, with a BS degree in Organizational Management and an MBA in Health Care Administration. Writing gives her the outlet she needs to live in the fantasy world that is a constant in her mind.

Thank you for reading and supporting A.D.'s books. Please take a moment to leave a review of this work. You can find her online at:

Facebook: https://www.facebook.com/adjusticeauthor
Twitter: https://twitter.com/ADJustice1
Web: www.authoradjustice.com
Email: adjustice@outlook.com
Newsletter: http://www.subscribepage.com/adjustice

BOOKS BY A.D. JUSTICE

Steele Security Series
Wicked Games (Book 1)
Wicked Ties (Book 2)
Wicked Nights (Book 3)
Wicked Intentions (Book 4)
Wicked Shadows (Book 5, Date TBD)

The Crazy Series
Crazy Maybe (Book 1)
Crazy Baby (Book 2)
Crazy Love (Short Story)
Crazy Over You (Book 4, Date TBD)
Drive Me Crazy (Book 5, Date TBD)

Dominic Powers Series
Her Dom (Book 1)
Her Dom's Lesson (Book 2)

Stand-alones
Intent
Just One Summer (Stand-alone Novella)
Completely Captivated (Stand-alone, Date TBD)